DON'T GIVE UP

UNEXPECTED ANSWERS
TO MARITAL CHALLENGES

MEN ON THE
EDGE

GARY HOFFMAN

Don't Give Up!
Copyright © 2010 by Gary Hoffman

Requests for information should be addressed to:
Men On The Edge
PO Box 283
Trabuco Canyon, CA 92678
www.MenOnTheEdge.com

Available at:
>   www.Amazon.com
>   www.CreateSpace.com
>   www.MenOnTheEdge.com

Library of Congress Cataloging-in-Publication Data

Don't Give Up: Unexpected Challenges to Marital Challenges / Gary Hoffman.

>   p. cm. – Book One

>   Includes bibliographical references.

>   ISBN 0-9845421-0-8 (pbk.)

LCCN #2010913780

A Special Thanks

This book is dedicated to the men whose hearts were changed in the midst of marital crisis and, despite their pain, helped start the "Men on the Edge" and "Separated Men's" ministries at Saddleback Church. My deepest appreciation for the input and feedback from the hundreds of men in support groups, including Pastor Rick Warren, for your leadership, support, and inspiration week-by-week. Thanks to Glen Kreun, Executive Pastor at Saddleback Church, for putting up with our men's group late night meetings in your office for 15 years and for mentoring the leadership team throughout the years. A special thank you to Tommy Hilliker, Pastor of Support Groups at Saddleback Church, for your "catch and release" attitude, vision, and encouragement to start the Men on the Edge support group. Thank you Clyde "Clydo" Botzner, for your friendship and leadership for the last ten years and your continued coaching and support for Men on the Edge ministry. Thanks also to the web guys: Jim Zoval for setting up the www.MenOnTheEdge.com website and creating the graphics for the *Men on the Edge* curriculum, and Gary Dahl for the www.separatedmen.com website. Marc Brown, Mike Chambers, Greg Hamer, Gary Malurek, Scott Meacham, Alex Varela, and Sasson Yazdizaden, thanks for your friendship, leadership, and support that have meant a lot to me personally. Jeff Harris, pioneering the ministry with you was a step of faith in the right direction. Thanks to Darren Rude for your friendship and "out-of-the–box" thinking. I want to mention Russ Steele for the focused wisdom that you have brought to the "pioneers" of Men on the Edge and Mary Scherff, for your wisdom and discernment, attention to detail, counsel, and friendship through the years. My deepest thanks to David Fuchs for putting up with me day-by-day, driving you nuts…as we rewrote the *Men on the Edge* curriculum. Without your Godly inspiration, input, and dedication, this book would not be possible.

And keeping the best for last, to my beautiful bride, Faith. Thank you for your day-by-day prayers, support, and sacrifice to make Men on the Edge possible.

In his love,

Your humble servant, Gary

CONTENTS

MY STORY

My story begins when I had just turned 40 years old. I was doing everything I could to save my marriage, but the harder I tried to work on my marriage, the more my wife wanted out of it. It was Christmas of 1994. She said, "I just need to be happy." Translation: my hopes and dreams for my marriage were being shattered.

Several months earlier, my pastor, Rick Warren, was preaching a series that focused on knowing your purpose in life. I remember him mentioning "most people here on earth don't know why they exist." I wanted to be part of those who knew their purpose in life. I wanted to be part of the few that lived with a purpose in mind. Day after day, I prayed and challenged God to reveal his purpose to me. I was growing closer to God, but my world was unraveling before my very eyes. It was getting worse before it was getting better.

I prayed and challenged God repeatedly to "change me" and I assured him that I could handle the pain. Oh boy, what a ride! In January 1995, I joined the Separated Men's Group, a support group at Saddleback Church, in which I was one of six men who were seeing their lives and families being torn apart by a divorce we did not want. We were not perfect, far from that. But why was all of this happening to us?

I was baptized in February of 1995 at the Saddleback Church winter retreat. I was still struggling to see where God was in all of this. I learned that God was right there! Right there in the middle of it all! I just couldn't see him at that time. He was right there, comforting me in my pain, encouraging me in my fears, and giving me serenity in my frustrations. I slowly began to see God's plan unfold in front of me. I had faithfully been attending the Separated Men's Group every week, learning and growing, little by little. God eventually began to use me in the men's group, as well as in my everyday life. I was on a high—God's high. I felt as if I was on a 100-foot wave, focused on God for the very first time in my life.

Several months later, Pastor Glen Kreun, the executive pastor at Saddleback Church, asked me to help lead and mentor the Separated Men's Group. Lives were changed on a weekly basis, as we learned to serve each other in humility and transparency, all the while holding each other accountable. One of our group themes was "work on me, work on me, work on me." I stopped pointing to others, and stopped blaming others for my shortcomings and my character flaws. I had to "own my part" in my struggling marriage. Somewhere along my journey, I had to admit I was part of the problem and also part of the solution.

The desire to change, to grow up in maturity, and to have a better attitude is an inside job. I had to realize that it was not all her fault. I had to "own it." It was more about me and my heart condition than I was willing to admit at that time. I had to learn that this "God stuff" is a lifestyle, a life in action, in my family, and more importantly…in my heart.

After leading the Separated Men's Group for 13 years, I saw hundreds of men's lives changed from the inside out, one "heart transplant" at a time. Leadership teams were developed to bring men back on track, equipping them to live the lives they were meant to live. In 2007, we launched "Men on the Edge," a different support group that would proactively work with men who were facing marital challenges, while still married. This expanding ministry is a group of men dedicated to helping other men work on their marriages, men committed to learning how to become spiritual leaders in their home by growing and trusting God in their everyday decisions. Our vision is to see Men on the Edge reach out to help other churches start similar ministries.

Today, we have a team of men working behind the scenes to write, develop tools, and create a website (www.MenOnTheEdge.com) designed to help educate men who are struggling in their marriages and who want to become proactive with God, in the midst of their marital challenges.

Divorce is not the answer. We are learning that "the grass is greener where you water it." Thanks to the experience gained, men are now seeing that they were missing a major component in their homes—spiritual leadership. It was missing in my home as it is in most homes. No matter what may be going on, it is about today, and moving forward from where you are today. Start learning and growing to become the spiritual leader in your home that God intends you to be.

Statistics show that a staggering numbers of women are unhappy in their marriage and they are often the ones who initiate the separation or divorce. Problems in a marriage may stem from a variety of reasons. One overarching reason is the disregard and lack of application of biblical marriage principles in the home such as love and respect, a fact that leads to confusing and competing roles. Another cause is that couples don't have time for one another because both are working. You cannot attend to your spouse's needs if you have no time dedicated to it. The added stress and pressure on working couples and their marriage vows impedes the implementation of clearly defined responsibilities, such as, "if our mutual responsibility is to help one another with chores around the house, rearing the kids etc., how do we do that when there is not physical time to do it?" Consequently, most men will not be or are not equipped to be the "spiritual leader" God has called them to be. In most cases, God is simply not at the center of their homes, where he belongs.

Surveys clearly indicate the destructive aspect of divorce in people's lives. The ones who are affected most are the children. Their greatest scars and pains are relational and emotional. These consequences will lead to dysfunctional behavior in their adult life. Some statistics also show that where God is really at the center of the marriage, the divorce rate drops to only 1 in nearly 39,000 marriages or 0.00256 percent (Dr. Tom Ellis, Chairman of the Southern Baptist Council on the Family).

I am proud to be a part of a group of men who are dedicated to help others understand and learn what it means to be the "spiritual leader" of their home. Without a spiritual leader in the home, there will be emptiness, restlessness, and failure. This restlessness is also referred to as "emptiness," as the hole inside each of us is saying: "I just need to be happy." Only God can fill that hole. Letting God be at the center of your life, with his peace, his presence, and his purposes in your marriage, can fill that hole. God will give you the strength to resist temptations and the courage to persevere for a better marriage. Your number one tool in a challenging marriage is prayer. Simply put: you can't pray too much.

Change is hard for all of us. One thing I have learned through the years is that most of us resist change because it leads to unknown areas of life and we naturally fear the unknown. We resist growing up because it may cause some pain. Pain is uncomfortable. Sometimes it takes a lot of pain for us to "get it," to learn, to change into a better person and to grow.

I am now married to my beautiful wife, Faith, who jokes, "It is your species, Gary." We laugh and say "men are only dense between the left ear and the right ear, that's all." God wants us to get it and to grow up, no matter what it takes. I encourage you to not give up on your marriage. Instead, focus on God. Own your part of the shortcomings in your marriage and start to learn how to grow from this day forward. When you focus on God, you will become proactive with him in your marriage and the solutions slowly will begin to emerge.

She's not perfect, and neither are you! Why? Because Adam and Eve have already taken a bite of the forbidden fruit. Yes, we are their descendants. No matter what may be going on in your marriage, don't give up. Dig into God's promises for you, for your marriage, and ask God to reveal his purpose for your life, which he specifically designed for you before the world was even created.

I encourage you to allow accountability and transparency in your marriage, as well as in your life. Surrender your marriage to "God's plan" and his ways for a better tomorrow. Your marriage is worth fighting for.

The Wild Ride of Change and New Life

After my decision to live according to God's will, I was baptized. There was no accompanying bolt of lightning or anything like that, but God faithfully revealed my sins and started a process of cleaning up my life from the inside out. After asking for his forgiveness, I asked God to change me. Literally everything in my life seemed to have turned upside down—my business, my personal life, my relationships, my spirituality, and most of all, the poor attitude of my heart. My perspective on everything has changed since then. Everything in my life has taken on a different meaning and appears different to me.

By God's grace, I started to recover from my marriage separation and from my depression. Through the leadership and mentorship of several amazing Saddleback Church members, I started to understand the process that God had me going through. He was using my hang-ups, my hurts, and bad habits to guide and help other men who were struggling in their marriage. The mentors who helped me in the beginning were like guardian angels. They helped me understand most of the titles you will find in this book.

You may be asking yourself the following questions:

- How does one make sense of it all?
- What are the real marriage roadblocks?
- Where is your focus?
- Who are you?
- What to do if your wife is having an affair?
- Do you date while separated?
- Do you need a lawyer, a mediator, or a reconciler?
- Do you know how to deal with anger?
- How do you not waste your pain?

I thank God and the leaders at Saddleback Church who have encouraged me and helped me to grow. They have helped me discover that I am a child of God and that he cares about all the details of my life. When I was in the middle of the storm, God was right there in the midst of it all.

I can confidently assure you that God can and will use your tears and pain to help others, if you let him. My prayer is that you will find God's peace, presence, and joy no matter what you may be going through and that you discover his purpose and why you are here. I encourage you to learn and study Rick Warren's book, *The Purpose Driven Life* (Zondervan, 2002). Let God begin to show you the reason why he created you.

This is my story. In the next chapter, we'll turn the focus to your story. How did you get to this place we call "the edge"? More important—how can you get back to where you belong?

Today, the God-inspired, key principles of the Separated Men's Group are used to help men on a daily basis. What was originally written as a handful of principles to get through the pain of marital challenges or separation has evolved into the Men on the Edge ministry curriculum.

The *Men on the Edge* book series was developed as God put these lessons on my heart. They come not only from my life, but also from the lives of the hundreds of men who have grown through this program. Their lives have helped other men and inspired the book you are holding. Their growth has stemmed from their failures and their victories. God is the one who made them grow. To God goes the victory!

CHAPTER 1

MAKING SENSE OF IT ALL

Are you feeling numb…in shock? Are you asking yourself, "How did I get here?" Have you been and/or are you still angry, frustrated, ashamed, confused…filled with other feelings that you cannot explain? Where do you start when your marriage is struggling? Here are the topics we will cover in this chapter:

- **Your Choices: be Depressed, become Bitter, or get Better**
- **Games of the Mind**
- **Your Behavior**

Your Choices: be Depressed, become Bitter, or get Better

Life is full of choices. What do your current choices look like? Whatever path you choose to follow, be aware that it leads somewhere. Start with the end in mind. The possible ends are these: Be depressed. Be bitter. Or get better.

1. **Do you want to be depressed?** My guess is, probably not. Most people who get offended in life deny the offense (pretend it didn't hurt, even though it did). Sometimes, they blame themselves for the offenses of others. The problem with this is it will make you shut down emotionally and you will end up depressed and alone. The best way to avoid being depressed is to surround yourself with other men who will understand your pain, help you stop stuffing your negative feelings (which can lead to depression), and support you in a healthy way (a support group).

2. **Do you want to be bitter?** The Bible says that bitterness is a poisonous path that leads to the destruction of the relationships with those around you as well as self in the long run. Hebrews 12:15 says, *Keep a sharp eye out for weeds of bitter discontent. A thistle or two gone to seed can ruin a whole garden in no time* (MSG). The process of becoming bitter takes time, but stems

from a choice, sometimes unintentional. Here is how it typically works: you experience the hurt, then you tell and retell the story in your mind, trying to make sense of it all. You would excuse or accuse the offender and get obsessed with the offense, seeking revenge and withdrawing from others... pulling you deeper into the well of bitterness.

3. Or do you want to get better? I recommend this path and assume that it is your choice. This is obviously why you are holding this book in your hands. Everybody wants to live a better and more balanced life. In this chapter I will discuss what you need to do and how to go about doing it.

You must place any blame appropriately. Own your part of the problem.

In order to grow through the excruciating pains of marital challenges and identify what has gone wrong, you must place the blame of any offense appropriately. When someone offends you, it is naturally human to seek payment for the offense. The problem is that the person who offended you has no way to pay for it. What would you charge? Who would determine if the payment you seek is valid or even reasonable? The only way to "get better" is to "let go" of the right to get even and the right to get revenge. Then start a grieving process in light of forgiveness and eventual reconciliation (if possible). Conflict is a manifestation of humans' self-centeredness, that is, original sin. Your response will define forgiveness and give way to reconciliation. Forgiveness is a must for God's children. Reconciliation, however, is optional because it depends not only on the forgiver, but also on the heart condition of the offender. A positive outcome will only work if your focus is not on you, not on the offense, but on the way you can reconcile with the offender (if possible).

Are you ready to work on the heart of the problems—no matter how painful the process? As Pastor Rick Warren says, "the heart of the matter is a matter of the heart." How's your heart?

The only difference between "better" and "bitter" is the letter "i." I can choose if I want to hold on to the hurt, to seek payment for it, or move on in a positive way into the future, with hope for reconciliation. I have that choice. So, do you. You must place any blame appropriately. However, you must not make it about you.

"The heart of the matter is a matter of the heart." Rick Warren

Games of the Mind

Your thinking affects your behavior by passing through your emotions. The natural behavioral process is that we first think about something. Then we feel according to that thought (our thinking), and this leads us to act according to our emotion (our feeling). One of the most erroneous myths in life is that you can change how you feel—you can't! You cannot change how you feel, no matter how hard you try. What you *can* do is allow God to change the way you think, which directly affects your feelings. The only way to do this is by applying God's Word (the Bible) and God's will in your life. (God speaks to you through the Bible, a sermon, a small group / support group or circumstances around you, which you know are orchestrated by God). If you do it this way, your behavior will eventually be intentional and it will follow a healthier emotional and thinking path. The truth of the matter is that you cannot control how you feel, but you can do something to control what you think. Once you grasp God's truth, you will realize that you are free to live under his umbrella. If you step outside of the umbrella, beware of the consequences—it hurts!

Is it all about you?

When I was finally honest with myself, I realized that I had been faking my Christian walk.

The funny thing about it was that I thought I had walked across the line to change my life and turn it around. I thought I was living as a Christian, I thought I had accepted Jesus Christ into my heart, I thought that I was on higher ground. But inside I was still hurting big time. When I was finally honest with myself, I realized that I had been faking my Christian walk. *So be careful how you live. Don't live like fools, but like those who are wise. Make the most of every opportunity in these evil days. Don't act thoughtlessly, but understand what the Lord wants you to do* (Ephesians 5:15–17 NLT).

How can you make the most out of every opportunity, so that you can learn, grow and bless others?

In everything you do, put God first, and he will direct you and crown your efforts with success. Proverbs 3:6 (TLB)

What matters most to you? Is it your wife, your kids, sex, sports, your buddies, your big house, or your fancy car? Maybe it's your job, your investments, or the remote control? Where is God on your list?

When your priorities are out of whack, God is pushed to the side or he's not on the list at all. Life then becomes difficult to live because once again, it's all about ME...ME...ME. Instead of living a life "about ME, ME, ME," live your life asking God to change your heart and attitude, so that you can live it saying: "Work on me, work on me, work on me."

> **Life then becomes difficult to live because once again, it's all about ME...ME...ME. Instead, ask God to "work on me, work on me, work on me."**

Are you wrestling with this? Is God taking first place in every area of your life? Do you believe that none of this is your fault? Are you afraid to step across the line and get to know God? Are you to reluctant to change or afraid of it? Are you complacent in life and just getting by? Are you missing the mark, as I was for many years? Or are you fully devoted to learning and growing...to become all God would have you be? What would happen if you changed your priorities from "I want..." to "God wants..." Look at what Paul says about this in the book of Romans: *Give yourselves completely to God...use your whole body as a tool to do what is right...* (Romans 6:13b NLT).

Your Behavior

My pastor, Rick Warren, gave me permission to quote directly from one of his sermons. I heard him explain the relationship between our thinking and behaving as a process, in a very logical and effective way:

Pastor Rick Warren on "Your Behavior":

Rick Warren's Sermon Excerpt

1. All behavior is based on a belief.

Do you ever do something that you think is kind of out of character for you and you wonder, "Why did I do that?" You did it because you believed something at that particular moment and you believed that was the best or most beneficial thing for you to do. You always act on your beliefs. And when you do something, it's because you believe something at that time.

If you go out and get a divorce, it's because you believe something at that time. You're saying, "I believe that a divorce will cause me less pain than staying in this marriage." It may be a lie but you believe it. When a woman thinks or says, "I'm leaving my husband and I'm going to marry this other man because I believe that is what I should do," she just expressed the belief behind her behavior. It may be wrong, but she believes it now of the decision.

If you know somebody who's having sex outside of marriage, it's because they have a belief that is causing that behavior. So behind every behavior is a belief.

2.   Behind every sin is a lie that I believe.

When you sin, at that moment you may think that it is the best thing to do, but you've been deceived. You say, "I know God says to do this but I'm going to do 'something else.' " What are you doing? You are believing a lie and acting upon it. Behind every sin is a lie.

Then you start looking at the lies behind why you act the way you do. When you start dealing with those, you'll start seeing some change in your behavior.

Titus 3:3 says *At one time we too were foolish, disobedient, deceived and enslaved by all kinds of passions and pleasures.* When you live in sin, you're living in deception and believing a lie.

When people look at you, they don't see the lies that you're believing but they do see your behavior. They know that you're unfaithful. They know that you're uncommitted. They know all these things. The tough part is figuring out the lie behind the behavior. Why are you behaving in such a way? **The wiser you get in life the quicker you'll start seeing the lies.**

3.   Change always starts in the mind.

You've got to start with the lie that has been acted upon. You've got to start with the belief behind the behavior. The Bible says *Be transformed by the renewing of your mind* (Romans 12:2). The way you think determines the way you feel and the way you feel determines the way you act. If you want to change the way you act, you must determine the way you think. You can't start with the action. You've got to start with the thought. Thoughts determine your feelings and your feelings determine your actions.

4. To change we must change our beliefs first.

The battle for sin always starts in the mind. You've got to see the lie that you are believing. That's why Jesus said, in John 8:32 *You will know the truth, and the truth will set you free.* Why? Because to change, you must first see your faulty belief. You've got to see your misconception. You've got to see the lie that you are basing your behavior on. That's why when you know the truth (God's word and will for your life) it sets you free.

5. Trying to change your behavior without changing your belief is a waste of time.

If you try to change your behavior before your mind is renewed, it won't work. You must internalize God's word first.

Example: In your mind are your belief patterns. Every time you think about a belief, it creates an electrical impulse in your brain. Every time you have that thought again, it creates a deeper rut. For instance: Let's say you go out and buy a speedboat and it has an autopilot feature on it. You set the speedboat to go north with the autopilot. The boat will go north automatically. You don't even have your hands on the wheel. If you want to turn the boat around, there are two ways you can turn around. One, you can manually grab the steering wheel of the boat and visibly force it by sheer muscle power to turn around. You are "forcing" it to go south even though the autopilot is saying go north! So you are forcing it to go south. The entire time you are under tension because you are going against the autopilot. When you are under tension, you will soon get tired and let go of the steering wheel. The boat will automatically turn around and go back to the direction that it's programmed; north.

This is true in life. When people have learned something over and over, having been taught by society and the world's way of thinking, they're programmed to go this way. Let's assume someone says, "I want to break the habit of smoking." He's programmed that every time he gets under tension, he picks up a cigarette. One day he realizes, "This is killing me! I'm going to get cancer. I'm going to die early." He grabs the "steering wheel" and turns it around forcibly and throws the pack away and says, "I am going to quit!" He makes it a week without a cigarette, a week and a half, two weeks...but the whole time he's under tension, because he hasn't changed the programming in his mind. Inevitably, he is going to let go of the "wheel" and pick up a cigarette again.

That also happens with people on diets and other behavioral modifications. If you want to change radically and permanently, you have to do it the New Testament way, *Be transformed by the renewing of your mind* (Romans 12:2). Just saying: "I need to stop smoking... I need to stop doing this and that..." isn't enough. It isn't going to work. You've got to change the belief pattern.

It's not hard to obey Jesus when your mind is renewed. But it's impossible to obey when your mind is not renewed.

6. The Bible term for "changing your mind" is "repentance."

What do you think of when you hear the word "repent"? Do you think of a guy on the street corner with a sandwich sign saying "Turn or burn... you're going to die and fry while we go to the sky." You may think of some kind of a kook.

But in Greek, the word "repentance" is a wonderful word, "metanoia," which means "to change your mind." Repentance is just surrendering the way you think about something by accepting the way God thinks about it. That's all repentance is. Changing the way I think about something by accepting how God thinks about it is a paradigm shift.

God is in the paradigm shifting business, in the mind and heart changing business. He is in the repentance business. He can change minds, not just at the shallow level, but at a deep level. The level of beliefs and values. God wants to help you change.

7. You can't really change your mind on your own; the applied Word of God does it.

You need to study the Bible, hear the Word of God, and apply it to your life. Look at what God's Word says about that: 1 Corinthians 2:13 tells us, *We speak words given to us by the Spirit, using the Spirit's words to explain spiritual truths* (NLT). Remember, you don't change your mind, the applied word of God renews your mind.

8. Changing the way you act is the result, or fruit, of repentance.

Technically, repentance is not behavioral change. **Behavioral change is the fruit, the evidence, and the result of repentance.** Repentance is simply changing the way you believe (think). This is a misconception we have. **Repentance does not mean forsaking your sin.**

You cannot find a single Greek dictionary that says repentance has that definition—forsaking of your sins. That's not what it means. That's what we've taken it to mean. "Stop all your badness and begin all your goodness"—that's what society calls "repentance." That is not repentance. "Repentance," the word, simply means "change your mind." That's why the Bible says a couple of times in scripture, "God repented." Why? Did

God have to stop bad and start good? No, it simply means God changed what he was going to do. He changed his thoughts. He changed his mind.

It's not a matter of behavioral change. It's a matter of mental change. John the Baptist said in Matthew 3:8, *Produce fruit in keeping with repentance.* The fruit isn't repentance. The fruit is the results. He said, "OK, you've changed your mind about God, about Jesus, about life, about sin, about death, about yourself, about marriage and about what's important in life. Now let's see some fruit as a result of it." Paul said the same thing. He said, *I preached that they should repent and turn to God and prove their repentance by their deeds* (Acts 26:20). Repentance is not deeds. Deeds are the proof of repentance.

From Rick Warren's message "The Purpose of Preaching"

So, if your thinking will determine your behavior, it is paramount that you identify the negative driver (negative lies about yourself or your selfishness). Examples of the negative lies can be: "I am not good enough," "It's all my fault," "I am a bad person," or "I am a failure." They can cause you to be depressed and react negatively to others. Once you do that, you will be able to reset your autopilot, change your route, and redirect your actions by living in a way that will glorify God and live at peace with other people.

POINT TO PONDER

You must place any blame appropriately.
However, you must not make it about you.

After reading this chapter, what do you need to repent about?

_____

_____

_____

CHAPTER 2

WHAT IS SIN ALL ABOUT?

In this chapter we will look at what sin is about, where it originates, how it affects you and others around you. We will look at:

- **What Is Sin All About?**
- **Free Will and Poor Choices**
- **EGO**
- **How Badly Do You Want A Solution?**

What is Sin All About?

One night in the middle of a group session, I threw out a question: "What is sin?" It's one of those words that can put people off, mostly because we don't understand it or its definition. But once we understand what sin is about, then we can begin to come to grips with it in our lives. One definition for sin is: "sin is turning away from God and disobeying the teaching or commandments of God." Through our discussion, we drew the conclusion that sin is a word, a thought, or an action against the moral law of God and that it could include any of the following:

1. The desire of the eyes
2. The desire of the flesh
3. The pride of life

We also drew the conclusion that God does not originate sin; the hearts of men do. The Bible says in 1 John 2:16, *For everything in the world—the cravings of sinful man, the lust of his eyes and the boasting of what he has and does—comes not from the Father but from the world.* Just look at the following examples of sin on the next page and you'll see that the list is a long one:

Pride	Greed	*Adultery*	Cheating
Ego	*Impatience*	Stealing	*Lack of Humility*
Fear/Worry	Unforgiveness	*Selfishness*	Ungodly Character
Unloving	*Inapropriate Anger*	Unfaithfulness	*A Hidden Agenda*
Anxious	Sexual Addiction	*Dishonesty*	Controlling

Sin always hurts someone. Harold McWhorter's song "Sin Will Take You Farther" (©Homeward Bound Music, BMI) says it like this:

> Sin will take you farther than you want to go
> Slowly but wholly taking control
> Sin will leave you longer than you want to stay
> Sin will cost you far more than you want to pay

It separates us from God and others. It can feel like fun in the midst of the moment, but sin has consequences in your life—consequences that are usually more intense and less fun than what you experienced in the midst of the moment of sin. Sin pulls you away from God and from all he has designed for you, including the people you love. Sin gradually creeps into your life. You slowly unplug from God and from your godly friendships. Sin creeps in the back door, draws you away from God, and pushes you into the hands of Satan.

> **Sin always hurts someone...**
> **It separates us from God and others.**

Here's another way I once heard it said: "A rationalized lie is where you stretch or twist the truth to support your hidden agenda."

If you know something you're doing is wrong but you continue doing it anyway, you are on the wrong path. You are on the path that will lead to destruction. You are free to sin, but be aware of the consequences. Once the sin has been committed, you no longer have the freedom of choice. The consequence is inevitable and is part of God's discipline. You reap what you sow and that is a universal principle. You're free to sin or not to sin, but you're not free to choose the consequences of your sin.

Free Will and Poor Choices... What's That All About?

"A rationalized lie is where you stretch or twist the truth to support your hidden agenda."

Do you ever wonder if God just puts up with you, just tolerates your selfishness, your pride, your anger and other inappropriate behavior? God wants us to do what is right; but most of us usually don't. We continue in a reactive mode: reacting to other people's behavior, including our own. Yet, when we genuinely love, we become **proactive** and don't need to react. Many times, when we react, it is out of anger. We tend to continue to make the same poor decisions and stay in an unhealthy and reactive mode. We may have done this for years and possibly learned it from our parents or others in our past. Many times we are just existing, just getting by in life, day by day, week by week—without love.

You might have had periods during which you tried to change a major character flaw on your own. This could be a New Year's resolution or a personal challenge to try and stop lashing out in anger or whatever. The sad fact is that most of the time you've failed in fulfilling the positive change. Why do you keep on failing at this? In Romans 7, Paul talks about this: *I know I am rotten through and through so far as my old sinful nature is concerned. No matter which way I turn, I can't make myself do right. I want to, but I can't. When I want to do good, I don't. And when I try not to do wrong, I do it anyway. But if I am doing what I don't want to do, I am not really the one doing it; the sin within me is doing it* (Romans 7:18–20 TLB).

> *Are you reacting with a "yes, but"?*
> *That's called rationalizing your sins.*

God gives us the free will to sin, even the free will to rationalize the sin and say, "Oh, it's not my fault" or "I did it because…it's someone else's fault." Be aware that God hates the sin, hates the poor choices we make. He hates the poor decisions we make in the heat of an argument. Yet, he still loves us in spite of our character flaws, in spite of our poor choices and in spite of our sin. Free will is why you are here on earth; it is what it is all about. You have free will to choose a better path, to make a better decision to obey God. You also have free will to humbly accept God's ways;

humbly admit that you don't have all the answers and that you need God's help to make better permanent choices.

> *God gives us the free will to sin, even the free will to rationalize the sin and say, "Oh, it's not my fault" or "I did it because…someone else's fault."*

Free will is a gift from God to every man and woman. He gives you the opportunity to choose between right and wrong. If you choose right, you choose his path and receive his wisdom. If you choose wrong, you will fall out of fellowship with God and separate from his perfect will for your life. That's probably where you are right now. I encourage you to seek God's help today, reconnect with him, and receive his perfect will, while it is still called "today." Ask for God's help in your daily problems and correcting your character flaws. Pray that it will be God's power in the situation and God's wisdom in your life that helps you change for a better outcome.

> *Free will is a gift from God to every man and woman, so that God permits you to choose between right and wrong.*

EGO (Edging God Out)

EGO is on display when you prioritize your own selfish agenda and is definitely a sin. It has serious implications; both spiritual, as well as practical. The Bible says that we should not only look after our own, but others as well. That includes your wife.

> *Each of you should look not only to your own interests, but also to the interests of others.* Philippians 2:4

This verse clearly explains that ego has no place in God's kingdom or family. Conversely, what is expected of you is precisely the opposite. Lay your selfish needs and wants aside, so that you can satisfy the needs of those around you. Your biological family, family by marriage, or church family are all part of this equation. The apostle Paul wrote in 1 Timothy 5:8, *Anyone who neglects to care for family members in need repudiates the faith. That's worse than refusing to believe in the first place* (MSG).

Ask yourself: "Is it all about me? Am I pushing God and his people to the side? Do I have a hidden agenda? What am I sold out to?" You may be a lot like me. I wasn't a bad guy, but I was not living like a Christian should, nor was I living a healthy lifestyle. Yes, I had been going to church for a long time. I knew the right words and I thought I had the right friends. I had acquired many possessions, the big house, and the latest toys with all the bills to prove it. But I was still missing the mark and I had no idea why I was still feeling empty at times. It seemed as if something was missing... but what? Was I simply going through the motions of Christianity, without a real relationship with God? So...where are you?

I remember that I felt torn between my unhealthy patterns and what I should really do. I had friends at church that would try to influence me in a positive way, while other "buddies" would try to pull me away towards a destructive lifestyle that would hurt my relationships and me. For an extended period, it's as if I was walking along the top of a tall wall, with my hands spread out as far as I could spread them. My "buddies," would be on one side and a handful of Christian friends on the other. I wanted the best of both worlds. I didn't see it at the time, but I was definitely not living with God at the center of my life. I wasn't involved in a Bible study. I was not in a men's group and I would only call on my Christian friends when my marriage was in trouble or when I needed someone to pray for me. When I thought about it, I only had two or three Christian friends that I could count on to pray for me at any time. But I had a lot of "buddies" and the tug of war between those two worlds was real. The "buddies" were pulling me away from a healthy marriage and lifestyle with my wife and son through golf, sports, fishing, or other distractions; my real friends wanted me to spend time with them, so that they could hold me accountable and help me heal and grow. The real friends were the ones who really cared. Are you wrestling with God? Do you believe that none of this is your fault?

Are you wrestling with God? Do you believe that none of this is your fault?

God wants more than just your heart. He wants all the areas of your life. He wants you to give him every problem, every thought, and every decision in your life. This is a concept that dates from biblical times. In the Old Testament, Moses wrote the following: *This is what the Lord your God wants you to do: Respect the Lord your God and do what he has told you to do. Love him. Serve the Lord your God with your whole being* (Deuteronomy 10:12 NCV).

As you grow in your character, will there be pain and suffering? Sure there will. But don't run from the pain. Sometimes things need to get worse before they can get better.

> *God wants your heart. He wants all the areas of your life. He wants you to give him every problem.*

Pain is a normal part of relationships. It is also a normal part of growth. Have you ever heard the saying: "No pain, no gain"? Sometimes the pain is so great that we would do almost anything to avoid it. Nobody likes pain. It causes us to turn to destructive behaviors (such as working long hours, hanging out with buddies, drinking, smoking, pornography, sports, drugs, etc.) You must understand that these vices only provide a temporary escape from the pain. They can provide an escape, but not a solution.

God wants us to learn that there is a purpose for pain. Pain is not in vain. He can teach us through our pain. The sooner we accept our need for God and that he is the only place where we will find significance in life, the sooner the pain will make sense and become more bearable. The only way to grow and heal is to face the source of the pain head on. Stay with the pain, learn from it, and invite God to share the reasons for it with you. We will discuss more about pain in Chapter 17.

> *The sooner we accept our need for God and that he is the only place where we will find significance in life, the sooner the pain will make sense and become more bearable.*

Do you know why we feel pain, why we sin and why we do the things we don't want to do? It's related to the way we process information and the way that we believe what we are doing is best for us. Sometimes, we deceive ourselves because our hearts and our minds are not aligned with the truth.

How Badly Do You Want a Solution?

How badly do you want to grow and understand your part in your marital challenges? Is it time for you to stop blaming someone else? If you want God to make a difference in your life, you have a decision to make.

You need a relationship with God, in order to understand God's plan and embrace the truth to change. Find out who God wants you to be. You may be feeling pain right now, but God's will for your life is for you to live an abundant life. He wants you to have a life of hope and a relationship with him. The apostle John wrote Jesus' words: *My purpose is to give life in all its fullness* (John 10:10b TLB). You will find the fullness of life that God intends for you in the expression of a life driven by a God-given purpose. Discover your talents, put them to work in a local church, and enjoy the ride.

Writing down your pain will externalize it and help you to share it with your support system (counselor, small group etc.). Start today and write it down in a journal or the *Don't Give Up* workbook.

Write about your pain. What are you feeling? Why are you feeling it?

Take a moment right now and pray. Ask God to help you find godly men to support you, the right Bible study to fellowship with, a Christian counselor to help you understand about God's truth and the right local church to connect with. Start making a difference today.

Warning: This will require courage, discipline and trust. It's the only way to advance in a healthy pattern of life and start to recover. Start with God and his team. He has instituted the church to help humanity reconnect with him. That's where you need to go for help.

Discipline yourself for the purpose of godliness.
1 Timothy 4:7 (NASB)

Is the pain bad enough to make you say, "I've got to live life differently, it just hurts too much"?

POINT TO PONDER

Are you wrestling with God?
Do you believe that none of this is your fault?

What sin has brought you to the situation you are in today?

_____

_____

_____

CHAPTER 3

ROADBLOCKS

FACING FACTS: What Are The Roadblocks to a Healthy Marriage?

As much as it may hurt, if you don't identify your problems, you can't begin to solve them. After all, you can't get rescued from the edge of the cliff if you're blind to the fact that you're on the edge. Step number one in getting away from the edge, is identifying the issues that have led you to where you are today.

Most relational roadblocks originate in wrong thinking, selfishness, and/or miscommunication. We do not communicate clearly, therefore, we do not know about each other's feelings nor how to meet them. The results are that we become overwhelmed with feelings of anxiety, resentment, and guilt. This is a spiritual problem.

...You can't get rescued from the edge of the cliff if you're blind to the fact that you're in trouble.

Be careful, or your hearts will be weighed down with dissipation, drunkenness and the anxieties of life, and that day will close on you unexpectedly like a trap. Luke 21:34

The theme of this chapter can be stated in one sentence: Roadblocks begin with a wrong belief, which leads to behaviors and feelings that deny us the satisfaction of our deep personal needs. God provides for all our needs. The problem is that sometimes we are not happy with his free provisions and believe that we know what our needs are better than he does.

Let us think about Adam and Eve for a minute. God provided for all their needs: food to eat, air to breathe, and a mate to procreate (and have fun) with. That was their bubble, it had the parameters that God wanted them to live by. In effect, God says: "If you trust me as your provider (and not yourselves), you will experience an abundant life." If they had stayed within the "bubble of God's provisions" they (and we) would have experienced the abundant life. But they did not stay within the bubble—it was not enough for them. They thought they knew better. But did they?

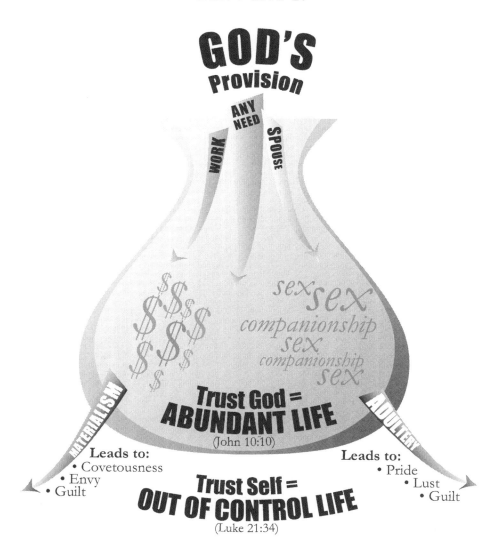

God had made it very clear that certain behavior was unacceptable (eating the fruit from the tree of knowledge of good and bad). Eating from the forbidden tree was considered outside of God's provision (the bubble) and would lead Adam and Eve to declare that they want to trust themselves and not God. Life would be "out of control."

If we choose to trust God as our provider versus trusting just the provision, we will be protected and less prone to suffer physical, psychological, and spiritual ailments.

Let's look at the graphic on the left. At the top, we see God's provision pouring down. It comes in many different shapes and quantities: work, spouse, finances—any provision. Provision that comes from God is not to be worshiped because that will get us into trouble as well. We must worship the provider, not the provision. While trusting the provider is good, you may not feel it is sufficient. In that case, you must also trust that the quantity provided will be enough to satisfy your need. And we must be grateful (content). If we fail to trust that it is enough and adequate, we will fall into the traps of anxiety, resentment, and ultimately, guilt.

Let's take the example of the provision of work. Work provides me with money, which I like because it enables me to live a comfortable lifestyle. If I fail to be content with the fruit of my work (money), I may become anxious that I may not have enough for tomorrow and look to fill my want with more work (outside of God's provision). I'm in danger now of falling for the sin of envy or covetousness or greed. The end result is that I will feel guilty (because I am).

Let us take the example of your spouse. If you resent the spouse that God has given you, or resent God for giving you that spouse—for whatever reason it may be—you might leave the "provisions bubble" and look for an additional mate outside of your marriage. This leads to the sins of lust, selfishness or even adultery. Ultimately, it will also lead to guilt.

The problems of resentment, guilt, and anxiety seem to be the three central underlying disorders in all personal problems and they exist because we think incorrect thoughts, which lead to sin outside of God's plan. The solution is to stay inside God's bubble for his provision and stay under God's umbrella for his protection.

Look at the bullet points below. Start to uncover some of today's roadblocks and establish some immediate goals:

Name the Problems

The starting place to solving a problem—especially a relational problem—is identifying the issues at their root, discovering the hidden issues. On the next page are a few steps to help you start.

TODAY'S ROADBLOCKS	GOALS FOR TOMORROW
It's all about you.	Start to care about your wife
You don't know your wife's needs.	Discover your wife's needs
You don't listen to your wife.	Learn to listen & empathize with her
No personal relationship with God	Become intimate/personal with God
Not trusting God will provide	Learn contentment/grow spiritually
You want to be your own god	Let go and let God
You are too busy	Learn to balance your life

1. **Pray.** God is the Master of relationships. In fact, he created them. Ask God for guidance in your relationships and with your uncovered issues. Pray that he puts those issues on your heart and gently allows you to see what they are. Pray to God to soften your heart as well as your wife's. Ask God for the ability to listen to and empathize with your wife so that you may get in tune with her emotions. Pray that he would reveal what is lying underneath the surface.

2. **Seek to understand your wife before being understood.**

Why do people act and react the way they do? Any normal human being's most basic needs include the need for significance and to feel loved. In order to stay emotionally healthy, these needs must be met. Living within God's provision says that there is nobody more appropriate to meet those needs than a spouse. You may not realize it, but you came into your marriage as a bundle of emotions, the sum of your emotional experiences as a child and a young adult. So did your wife. Here's the million-dollar question: Does your wife feel significant and loved by you? The question is not whether you love her. Does she *feel* that you love her? She will find significance in that emotion of love and acceptance. Here's another question: Do you feel significant in her eyes and do you feel loved and respected by her? The question is not whether she respects you but whether you *feel* respected by her. If the answer to any of these questions is "no" or "I don't know" or "maybe," it is no wonder that you are facing relational difficulties.

3. Ask your wife. First, it might be necessary and helpful for her to hear from you that you don't have it all together. Just admit it; let go of your pride and be humble. Ask her what her perspective is on the current situation. Do so without judging or even responding. Be slow to speak and quick to listen. Let her share and refrain from interjecting anything, even if she says that she has "told you a million times." Let her know that she has your undivided and non-judgmental attention and you really want to hear her out. Say, "Would you please tell me, one more time, how you see our situation?" Show her that you care and that you earnestly want to listen to her point of view. Do your best to listen and not say anything. It is likely that emotions will cloud your thinking or confuse your hearing, so take a moment and jot down some ideas to review later. Don't use the written down ideas against her. They are just for you to reflect on and to help you understand, without your emotions cluttering your thoughts.

Million Dollar Question: *Does your wife feel significant and loved by you?*

The starting place in solving a problem—especially a relational problem—is identifying the issues at their root.

4. Now ask yourself:

What specifically are the issues causing your marital challenges? You might say that it is sex or something else that is obvious. The issue is not obvious; otherwise, you would have "obviously" been able to resolve it. One important clue for most men: sex is not the problem. Rather, it's a symptom of other underlying issues, much deeper problems.

- **Do you know the root of the problem (underlying issue)?**
- **Have you faced the issues head on?**
- **Is God in your marriage formula?**
- **Do you trust God or do you prefer to trust in his provision?**
- **Can you admit that you don't have it all together?**
- **Can you confide with a trustworthy and "safe" male friend?**

The reason that marriage is difficult is because the way to make it work is not obvious. Good marriages don't just happen. A good marriage requires many things such as time, effort, grace, forgiveness, trust, respect, and intentional love. Intentional love…what does that mean? It means that you will sacrificially love her (even when you don't feel like loving or when she is unlovable). Intentional love is what your wedding vows were all about.

Is your commitment and dedication to your wife still in line with the vows you made when you married her? You promised in front of God and others to love, honor, and cherish her, "until death do us part." Right? Think about what that promise meant to you and what you think it meant to her. If you don't know what it meant to her, ask her. You might also be surprised to find that you have not been faithful to your vows, in her opinion. Most men aren't. Men tend to get off track after the wedding ceremony by becoming complacent or changing their focus from her, the prize that is now "conquered," to work or other "projects."

When you were dating, do you remember how you pursued her? She does, and she liked it—that's one of the reasons she married you. You relentlessly wanted to be with her while you were courting her. When and why did that stop? She probably noticed that the pursuit ended and she became disillusioned with marriage (you), finding herself alone, abandoned and neglected. Who caused those feelings? The answer may be obvious to her. It is not to you, because as men, we usually don't ask ourselves the pertinent questions that consider the feelings of others. You may have triggered her emotions and feelings of loneliness, abandonment, and neglect. When we fail to ask the right questions, we will fail to get the right answers. When you focus on what she has done wrong or on how you got hurt and disappointed with life, you won't get anywhere and neither will your marriage. Your focus needs to be on your responsibility and how to carry it out within the parameters of God's design for marriage. What is your responsibility? To love your wife!

When we fail to ask the right questions, we will fail to get the right answers.

There are two kinds of issues: the obvious ones and those underlying the surface. The underlying issues cause many of the obvious issues and destructive behavior in your life. In order to resolve relationships that have gone south, one must dig deeper into the causes of alienating behavior. What is the root of that behavior? Below is a list of issues that you might identify with. Typically, money, sex, children, or in-laws cause most obvious issues in a marriage. These are legitimate spousal concerns and can be immediate causes for problems in a marriage. However, the resolutions reside not in the immediate causes, but in the identification of the root causes. What happened in your youth that might be causing you to act in a certain way in your adulthood, which may cause you to rationalize a hurtful behavior?

Check the possible roadblocks in your marriage:

Spiritual

- ☐ You are not the spiritual leader in your marriage
- ☐ No spiritual intimacy
- ☐ You want to control your wife and others

Love

- ☐ Love and respect issues
- ☐ Failing to cherish your wife
- ☐ Trust issues
- ☐ Failure to affirm/appreciate her
- ☐ Your wife feels she is not number one in your life
- ☐ No affection towards your wife
- ☐ Not physically accepting your wife's body
- ☐ No physical intimacy

Character

- ☐ Selfishness
- ☐ Compulsiveness
- ☐ Co-dependency issues

Communication

- ☐ Lack of clear communication
- ☐ Not listening to your wife
- ☐ Not appreciating your wife's unique qualities
- ☐ Lack of verbal intimacy

Other

- ☐ Verbal and/or physical abuse
- ☐ Financial issues
- ☐ Spending too much time at the office
- ☐ Not helping with the kids
- ☐ Addictions (porn, sex, drugs, alcohol, etc.)
- ☐ Issues with in-laws
- ☐ Blended family issues
- ☐ Allowing in-laws to interfere in how you rear your children

The underlying issues are usually difficult to identify and are often the cause for some of our behavior and poor decisions. But they are not the only root. There is a more important cause to our problems and behavior. The way we see the world around us and how it functions can influence our belief system. I remember that this was true for me. Whatever was happening to me was someone else's fault, not mine. I was an angry and defensive little grown-up boy, who did not receive the love he required or expected as a child. The blame was conveniently placed on my parents. However, I was no longer a child. I was a grown man who made his own decision to have a family. Therefore, I had to assume the responsibility of my problems. To a certain degree, it is true that we are the sum of our experiences from our childhood and youth. But as adults, we must start to assume responsibility for our actions and stop blaming others (wife, parents, in-laws, etc.).

We are the sum of our experiences but eventually we must assume responsibility for our actions and stop blaming others.

The greater cause of your marital problems is not your youth or any part of your past, but the way you think and the way you view the world around you. The way you think and the way that you perceive the world allows you to set false expectations of receiving without giving. The universal principle of sowing and reaping is active in a marriage relationship. You cannot get anything out of it without putting something into it first.

As you move forward in your journey, you will hopefully begin to understand that love and respect are the foundations for a healthy marriage. Look back at the list previously outlined and see if anything on the list is a clear or potential problem in your relationship. Write it below or in a journal. Identifying your true root problems in writing is another critical starting step toward resolving issues in your marriage. The foundation of a healthy and functional marriage lies in love and respect. Men are to love their wives and wives are to respect their husbands.

The greater cause of your marital problems is not your youth or any part of your past, but the way that you think and the way you view the world around you.

POINT TO PONDER

Million Dollar Question:
Does your wife feel significant and loved by you?

Is God in your marriage formula? Yes or no?

_____

_____

_____

CHAPTER 4

THE ART OF LISTENING

Listening needs to be done in an intentional fashion. A dialogue is not a series of two monologues. Rather, it is an interactive motion in which both parties speak and listen, but not at the same time. How well do you listen?

You need to change the way that you think, act, and communicate, so the focus is on *your* thinking, your action and your communication. What you should not change—or try to change—is your wife. Only she can change herself, with God's help. All that you can change is yourself and the way you interact. Take the focus off of her and place it upon God and on what he wants you to do and respond. Don't try to change your wife!

At this moment, you may not be sure what to do. As you struggle to determine the roots of the problems, know that there is one thing you can do. Start working on your attitude. Look at what author Chuck Swindoll says about attitude:

> *Wherever you are, no matter what might be happening in your marriage, start living to show your wife that it is not about you, but about your marriage. Listen to her and serve her so that she may feel entitled to her emotions; that her emotions are validated, recognized, and protected.*

Ignoring the problems won't make them go away. You may have heard it said that the definition of insanity is to keep on doing the same thing while expecting different results. Whatever you do, don't keep on doing the same thing. Start moving forward and take action steps that will lead you to a healthy behavior and a healthy marriage—one that is proactive with God in your recovery season. You might feel that sometimes you are taking two steps forward and one step back. You may question whether the process is working. But two steps forward and one back still means that you have made one step forward, which represents recovery and growth. It may be painful, but it is worth it.

Maybe you're walking on eggshells around your wife or she feels like she's walking on eggshells around you. One of you may be feeling that he or she is not living up to the spouse's expectations. If she's the one walking on eggshells, I encourage you to try to see yourself and your marriage through her eyes. Pray for clarity to truly make sense of the roots of your marital problems. Seeing clearly may be tougher than you imagine, but with God's help, the root causes will start to become apparent. It's critical that you start today. Proverbs 3:5–6 says, *Trust in the Lord with all your heart, and lean not on your own understanding; in all your ways acknowledge him and he shall direct your paths* (NKJV).

> *Listen to her and serve her so that she may feel her emotions are validated.*

Start by listening to your wife. Hear her. You don't need to necessarily agree with her, but at least listen. In *10 Great Dates to Energize Your Marriage* (Zondervan 1997), experts David and Claudia Arp tell us, "Feelings are neither right nor wrong; they simply are." A counselor at our church says it this way: "Feelings are real, but they don't always reflect reality." That means that your wife's feelings are valid no matter what your perception of them might be. It means that your feelings are also valid, no matter what her perception of them might be. I can't tell you how liberating it was for me to realize that truth. Seek to understand your wife's pain, confusion, and frustration. Put yourself in her place as much as you can and try to empathize with her and sympathize with her feelings.

How to Effectively Listen

Effective listening means to hear what your wife is saying. Again, you do not have to necessarily agree with her, but you must hear her in order to understand her.

Listening is a skill that I encourage you to acquire. God gave us two ears and one mouth. Maybe he wants us to listen twice as much as we speak. Unfortunately, most of the time spent in "communicating with a spouse" is not spent listening, but talking. Many of our habits are bad ones that we need to unlearn. It's hard to admit it, but most of us men have poor listening skills. Since our sandbox days, we were raised to solve problems and that usually involves tools or brute force.

> **Listening to the opinion or perspective of others is generally not our natural response.**

Our natural need is to be honored and respected. We need to "fix" her, no matter how she views it. This is our "fix-it" cap, which is not what your wife usually needs. She needs her man to listen, pay attention, and nurture her feelings, thoughts, and emotions. Our "fix-it" attitude does not meet her needs. It only reflects our own needs.

Women on the other hand are more relational by nature. Their natural need is to communicate and to be loved because it helps them feel secure. It is what I call her "feels with me" cap. She needs her hubby to feel her emotions. In other words, "taste them…smell them…feel them." She needs her husband to empathize with her. Her emotional well-being depends on the very fact that you are able and willing to understand what she is feeling.

When you come home from a long day's labor, your wife may start sharing problems she's had during the day—with the kids, work, or whatever. She may present the issues from a number of different perspectives. She may even offer a few different solutions and ask you which one you think is best. It is imperative that you make the most out of this opportunity.

It's critical to mirror back what you hear from your wife—not just what you think you hear.

This moment is critical for you to understand that your wife only wants to be heard and understood by you. She's not intentionally trying to trick you. However, you, being the problem-solving man that you are, may want to fix her problems. She's not necessarily looking for a solution; she just wants to be heard and empathized with. So, listen reflectively. Mirror what you hear her say with your own words back to her and then ask her if you understood her correctly. That is empathy. That is what she needs.

You may say to her, "Is this what I am hearing you say?" Then repeat back to her what you understood her to say. This is a very important step in your communication habits. It's critical to mirror back what you hear from your wife—not just what you think you hear. Allow her to correct you without getting defensive. Stay calm as she speaks. When you do, God often opens the eyes of her heart, allowing her to feel that you are not only present, but that she is actually being heard and appreciated. She needs that. Hear her out; be a good listener before you respond.

A friend of mine whom I will call Mike asked his wife to tell him if there was anything he could do to help "fix" what was wrong between them. She told him, "Nothing! Don't even try…that's all you ever do… fix, fix, fix. It would take a miracle from God to make me come back to you, because you don't focus on my needs or my emotions…you just don't hear what I have to say…all you want to do is know what you can fix." This time, Mike heard her loud and clear. He began praying for a miracle, but he had to change his ways (attitude) first. He had to learn to listen and empathize.

Listening to your wife doesn't mean you're going to like or agree with what she has to say.

Listening to your wife doesn't mean you're going to like or agree with what she has to say. But if you fail to honestly listen to her, you can't even begin to work on what's wrong in your marriage. Why? Because you can't know her perspective if you don't listen to what she has to say about how she feels. You have to hear your wife's side of the story before anything can change. Even when you do, you're only starting. Consider it square one. Pray that God opens your eyes to see the truth, while it is in front of you. Pray that he will tune your ears so that you may hear the truth. Pray for God to soften your heart so that you will not lean on your own (biased) understanding, but lean on him and his wisdom.

What I'm presenting here is not rocket science, but simply good communication principles. Whenever others—your wife, your kids, or co-workers feel heard, understood and appreciated, they will feel more comfortable around you. They will learn to trust you and believe in you, because you are able to mirror back what their feelings are.

When you do, God often opens the eyes of your wife's heart, allowing her to feel that you are not only present, but that she is actually heard and appreciated.

Tools for listening

The S.O.L.E. of listening:
- **S** quarely face your mate
- **O** pen body postures
- **L** ean into your spouse
- **E** ye contact

Listening is an action:
- Listen with your eyes
- Listen with your ears
- Listen with your heart
- Listen to build up, not tear down

Everyone should be quick to listen,
slow to speak and slow to become angry. James 1:19

Do you see a man who speaks in haste? There is more hope for a
fool than for him. Proverbs 29:20

Keys for Good Listening

1. **Be Quiet and Listen**

   Allow group members to share, maybe 10 to 15 minutes each.

2. **Give the Person Speaking Freedom to Share**

   Help group members feel comfortable about sharing their true feelings.

3. **Be an Engaged Listener**

   Strive to understand the group member. Look at them while they talk and express interest.

4. **Help Minimize Distractions**

   Shut off cell phones, laptops, minimize noise in the meeting room, and avoid any unnecessary shuffling of papers.

5. **Be Empathetic as You Listen**

   Learn to care about the person in front of you!

6. **Be an Understanding Listener, Trying not to Interrupt**

   Allow the group member to share without interruption. Be patient and ask questions with interest and consider your timing.

7. **Don't Get Angry About What is Said**

   Do not let a group member get the best of you; be slow to anger, quick to listen.

8. Try Not to be Critical or Appear Judgmental

Try not to be confrontational or argumentative with group members, as group meetings are not the proper format for confrontation.

9. Ask Good Questions

Encourage sharing that will help lead group members to answer their own questions and promote thought-provoking dialog and sharing. You cannot solve a group member's problems. Learn that a secret to leadership is to ask good questions.

10. Let Others Share From Their Hearts

Again, stop talking so others can share from their hearts. As you learn the skill of listening from the heart, you will pass this valuable skill on to others through your example.

> *Learn the skill of listening rather interrupting others with your opinion.*

> HINT: *Most often, your wife is not looking for a solution. She just wants to feel heard and to feel empathized with. What she wants is your undivided attention.*

POINT TO PONDER

Listen to her and serve her so that she may feel entitled to her emotions, that her emotions are validated, recognized and protected.

Which of the "Keys for Good Listening" have you ignored?

_____

_____

_____

CHAPTER 5

FEELINGS:

Do They Reflect Reality?

While your wife is talking, she in the process of expressing her feelings, her emotions, or her situation. She wants your attention and to include you in that process. For that reason, you need to be 100 percent present physically and mentally. As your wife processes, she does not necessarily want you to solve the problem, but wants to be heard and listened to. If you're not sure, ask her clearly, "Is this something you want my opinion on, do you want me to find a solution, or do you want me to just listen?" Try it. You may be surprised at her response.

Feelings are real but they don't necessarily reflect reality.

These are the action steps to start moving forward. You now begin to hear your wife and learn about her heart condition without having to defend yourself. This is what your relationship needs in order for it to become healthier. The action steps for growth are removing the roadblocks identified at the beginning of this chapter.

Write down how you could do the following:

1. **How can I start to show care to my wife?**
2. **How can I learn to discover her needs and commit to meet them?**
3. **How can I learn to listen and empathize with my wife?**
4. **How can I start an intimate and personal relationship with God?**

Owning Your Part

The way to remove roadblocks is admitting that what needs to happen is an inside job: She is not the problem—the problem is a lack of clear communication and biblical focus on your marriage. There may be as many causes as there are consequences for this. What am I saying? You might be the one who needs to be worked on and not necessarily your wife.

You will learn that it is probably more about you and your part in the situation than hers.

I know a man whom we will call Robert. He and his wife had been going from counselor to counselor for over two years. Together, they had seen more than eight different counselors and Marriage and Family Therapists (MFTs). To each counselor, the husband presented his wife's problems and issues in such a convincing way that the problem was always focused on her. One counselor finally suggested that the man was at least 50 percent responsible for their marital problems and asked the husband to consider this vantage point. Robert did. As a result, they resolved their issues because he was able to own his own part of the deal. That was actually all that she needed him to do. If you are ignoring her feelings, that could be a cause of the situation. Your ignoring or neglecting her needs is a part of the problem. The fact that you cannot listen to her without being defensive is certainly part of the problem. The fact that God is not at the center of your marriage is obviously a problem. Here's a question for you: Is your behavior an inspiration to her? Do you model leadership and integrity or are you controlling, loud, and self-serving? You cannot change your wife. The only person you can change is you. What you can do is model a positive attitude that she will likely want to imitate. If you are able to change your attitude for it to become more attractive to her, she will naturally be attracted to you.

You must ask God to work on you rather than expecting him to work on her.

It's OK to ask God to work on her, but focus on what needs to change in you, first. Then, put your focus on God and not on her. Remember the theme of our *Men On the Edge* book series: "Work on me. Work on me. Work on me."

> *Will you start caring about how she feels?*
> *Roll up your sleeves and start digging into the problems.*

The Game of Empathy – Reflect Back What You Hear and Help Her Feel Understood

Even if you don't agree with your wife, listen to what she is saying about her view of the problems in your marriage. It may sound like all she's doing is blaming you or pointing out where you need to change, but hear her point of view and try to do so without being defensive. Try to understand and value what your wife is feeling. This is called empathy and women love it! Too many men ignore their wife's feelings, yet these feminine feelings are what drive them and give them a sense of identity. If a husband fails to empathize with his wife's feelings, she will feel unimportant and insignificant. Consequently, she will gradually detach from her uninterested and seemingly indifferent husband. If your marriage is shaky but you are still together—or even if you are separated—there is still hope. It is not too late for you. But you must be willing to hear her out—genuinely hear with your heart what your wife is saying. Empathize without attacking her or her feelings. Most men do not value their wife's feelings. Don't put them down. They are important to her.

If getting better is what you really want—and it probably is or you wouldn't be reading this book—you must understand what the problems are.

> *No matter how much it hurts to own your own part, don't deny it, don't ignore it—own it! If you own your part of the issue, you will begin moving away from "the edge."*

You will stay on the edge until you start looking at life differently and learn to listen and empathize with your wife's feelings.

Feelings are Neither Right nor Wrong

Your wife may say, "I don't love you anymore." She is feeling that she is not in love, that she doesn't love you, that she cannot and will not ever love you again, but she is merely describing a feeling. Feelings are neither right nor wrong—they just are.

However, love is more than a feeling. It is a choice. It is a decision. Because love is more than a feeling, we should not base our behavior and lifestyle on the feeling that love produces. If the feeling (emotional state) produced by love affects your thinking and your being, then you will be inconsistent and driven by emotions rather than intentionally driven by reason and purpose. If falling in love causes you or your wife to react, then falling out of love will also cause you to react.

> *Love is not only a feeling; it is a decision that leads to a commitment that leads to an action that will bring the feelings.*

When we fall in love, that tumble is accompanied by a feeling, or many feelings, but it implies more. Real lasting love is a decision and a commitment long after the honeymoon feelings have faded. Love is a choice; it is an action. It is not something we just feel, it is something we choose to do.

In a heated marital crisis, it may seem as if the "emotional love switch" has been turned off, but that is only the emotional switch. Was the commitment, the choice or the decision ever there? Choice and decision go with the wedding vows commitment. Those were certainly present when you got married. But now, your wife says that she has had enough of you—your poor attitude, your anger, your coming home late, or your working too much, your indifference, or whatever.

It is also critical to acknowledge your own true feelings, to put words to them. Most men and women dismiss them and miss this part. I know that I did. We don't take the time to analyze, identify, and put words to our true feelings. Consequently, they are not in tune with their emotions and cannot resolve their issues, except to get angry and show frustration.

As noted earlier, your feelings are neither right nor wrong, they just are. According to marriage specialists and authors Claudia and David Arp, "Feelings are fragile and we must handle them with care. But if we can get to the real roots of the issues through sharing our true feelings in a loving and mutually safe way, then we can resolve the problem while strengthening our marriage instead of attacking each other." Once you put words on your feelings, you can start to deal with the unmet needs often hidden deep inside.

> *Love is a choice; it is an action. Love is not something we just feel, it is something we do.*

Categories of Feelings for Men

When asked how they are feeling, most men will respond with "fine" or "great." But do you really feel "fine"? Are you really doing "great"? We men have a tendency to mask our true feelings. Maybe it's the scared little boy inside trying not to reveal his insecurities, but it's a poor method of self-protection. We want to be seen as "tough guys," but the reality is that we are insecure and we do seek to be accepted by others in a broken world.

Men are the problem solvers in their own world, in their careers and in their families—yet we often don't take the time to analyze our true feelings in a situation or conflict.

What is making you tick or what are the real underlying motives in the situation? Don't be afraid to ask yourself these questions. Be honest with yourself. Become aware of your true inner feelings. I encourage you to identify your feelings by using the "one-word" feelings chart below.

Do any of these emotions describe how you are feeling? Notice that "fine," "great," and "OK" are not on the **Feelings List**. Pray for God to help you put words to your true feelings. Circle those that describe how you are feeling about your marriage right now and add any you do not see here.

I encourage you to be candid with yourself about your feelings and sympathetic with her about hers. Resist the temptation to watering down or minimizing the importance of feelings. Reach for honesty and transparency with yourself and your wife in order to discover the true nature of your feelings. It's the pathway to understand where you both are in the relationship, emotionally speaking. This is one of the ways to move away from the edge of the cliff and set your feet on higher and safer ground.

One-Word Feelings Chart

Angry	Numb	Scared	Lost	Sad
Frustrated	Overwhelmed	Hurt	Abandoned	Tired
Hopeless	Inadequate	Panicky	Bitter	Nervous
Insecure	Inadequate	Betrayed	Ambivalent	Trapped
Confused	Jealous	Embarrassed	Lonley	Anxious

If you want to resolve the challenges in your marriage, you will have to change the way you think, act, and communicate.

POINT TO PONDER

Feelings are real but they don't necessarily reflect reality.

What is your part in your marital challenges?

_____

_____

_____

CHAPTER 6

UNHEALTHY FOCUS

If you have been trying to change your wife, stop it right now. How does God expect you to love her? By changing her? Most men focus on women and most women focus on men. It is our natural inclination and interest. However, both are wrong because it puts our focus in the wrong place: on fallible, selfish, broken human beings. The primary focus should be on the origin of it all: God. God instituted marriage for human beings so that each could have a spouse. Your spouse is supposed to be an addition to your life but not the originator of it. Unfortunately, your spouse, who is supposed to become a complement of you, becomes a competition to your life because your focus is on her or your own selfish agenda.

Is your focus on everything that your wife does wrong? Or is it all about your and her shortcomings?

Write down the problems in your marriage. What are they? Is your focus on everything your wife does wrong? Or is it all about your and her shortcomings? Do you focus on her, what she does, what she says? Do you try to control her and her actions and whereabouts? The only way to change your wife, definitely and positively, is by loving her unconditionally and changing your focus. Keep it off of her and place it on God (first) and on what he has to say about marriage and relationships. How does God say that you will have a successful marriage? By doing it the way he designed it. The question becomes: How did he design marriage?

Each husband and each wife have a set of responsibilities and functions. Men and women are spiritually equal in front of God but that does not mean that their functions are equal. They are not. Men have a need that only God and wives can meet. Wives have needs that only God and husbands can meet. We get into problems when we look outside of marriage to meet our needs, because that is not how he designed it. When it comes to our needs, we must focus on God and no one else.

They are darkened in their understanding and separated from the life of God because of the ignorance that is in them due to the hardening of their hearts. Having lost all sensitivity, they have given themselves over to sensuality so as to indulge in every kind of impurity, with a continual lust for more. Ephesians 4:18–19

Ask yourself: Are you in a healthy, God-focused relationship or in an unhealthy, self-focused relationship? Here are some unhealthy examples… we've included samples in the graphic above, but the words can be exchanged with those in the list on the next page. They are all unhealthy behaviors.

Unhealthy Behavior

1. Manipulative behavior

2. Controlling behavior

3. Resentful behavior

4. Inappropriate anger

5. Demanding behavior

6. Conditional love

7. Assuming the responsibility of others

8. Wanting-to-get-even behavior

9. Focusing on your wife instead of on God

Unhealthy Behavior that Keeps You from Focusing on God

1. Manipulative behavior

A manipulative behavior shows that you are not happy with your wife and that you are trying to force her to your hidden agenda. Often you may not even be aware of these controlling motives. Your approach is subtle but sinful and destructive.

Don't try to manipulate, control, or change your wife. Don't be resentful, demanding...

2. Controlling behavior

A controlling behavior on your part means that you do not trust your wife, or whomever you are trying to control, and you feel the need to dominate that person. It could also mean that you are insecure and that you find significance in your "ability" to control someone else. It could be that your issue of control goes beyond your marriage and extends in other areas of your life: your professional life or with your friends, parents, kids, etc.

3. Resentful behavior

This is usually evidence that there are hurts in your past or present that have not been forgiven. This needs immediate attention such as seeking out a pastor, Christian counselor, or a safe men's group to work through this resentfulness. If you continue, it will lead to bitterness and potential depression.

4. Inappropriate anger

Anger will stem from other emotional areas. It is called a secondary emotion, usually fed by fear, confusion, frustration, or anxiety, or a combination of these. It is OK to get angry because sometimes it helps open the door to forgiveness. But when expressed, anger must be controlled in an appropriate time and place and for the appropriate reason.

5. Demanding behavior

The problem with demanding behavior is that it lacks love. Love in a marital relationship requires the husband to lead while serving and not expecting or demanding service from his wife or others.

6. Conditional love

If you do that, then I will do this…A man's love for his spouse should not depend on her. Let's suppose that she becomes sick and is unable to love you according to your expectations. Does that entitle you to stop loving her? You must love your wife without condition. That is how God designed your marriage.

7. Assuming the responsibility of others

There are responsibilities within the marriage and other relationships that are not yours. Nurturing co-dependent tendencies is destructive in any relationship. In a healthy relationship, each person should own their part of a situation. Learn to let others own their part or suffer the consequences.

8. Wanting-to-get-even behavior

This is the "You hurt me, therefore I will hurt you behavior." Revenge is unacceptable, although it is a natural tendency for all human beings to want it. Desiring to get even with someone fuels the path to resentment and bitterness. It's not healthy and will cause years of unnecessary pain and destruction.

9. Focusing on your wife instead of God

The only time when this is appropriate, is when it is for serving her or pleasing God. Your focusing on her first rather than focusing on God first will lead you down an inappropriate path. You will always be able to find fault, prejudice, or reasons to be resentful if your primary focus is either on her or on yourself.

Don't try to manipulate, control, or change your wife. Don't be resentful, demanding, or express inappropriate anger.

Is any of the above-mentioned behavior present in your relationship with your spouse? If it is, it shows that your focus is in the wrong place. Stop focusing on what she says and what she does or what she doesn't say and what she doesn't do. Let it go! Focus on God and on how you are to be with her in front of God. If you would honestly look at yourself and your behavior, would you agree that you need some improvement in the way you interact with her?

In an unhealthy marriage, the focus is rarely on God. If your wife throws mud, you will probably throw it back, with a little added on to it. Your goal should be to focus on God and what he has to say about the functions of husband and wife in a marriage. In Ephesians 5:33 it says, *However, each one of you also must love his wife as he loves himself.* Rise above the mudslinging. Strive to see her through the eyes of God. Learn to love your wife as God loves her.

In an unhealthy marriage, the focus is hardly ever on God.

POINT TO PONDER

Is your focus on everything that your wife does wrong? Or is it all about your joint shortcomings?

What do you focus on?

_____

_____

_____

HEALTHY FOCUS

Let's look at the positive side of your focus. Remember that when the focus is on God, you will be able to respond to your circumstances more peacefully, which will lead to a significant and balanced life. Look at the chart below, which shows the healthy focus. Rather than having the focus on your spouse or yourself, you now intentionally put it on God first. Listen to what he says through his Word (the Bible) and through prayer. Find God in the situation; discover his will for you and your marriage. As you look at the graphic below, what do you need to do, in order to focus on God?

Trust in the Lord with all your heart and lean not on your own understanding; in all your ways acknowledge him, and he will make your paths straight.

Proverbs 3:5–6

Where is Your Focus?

So how do you do it? How do you stay focused on God? Follow the suggestions below. These are the **how tos** that will lead you onto the right path. There are two visible ways to interact with God. They are both in a biblical passage known as "The Great Commandment." This passage says:

> *Jesus replied:* **"Love the Lord your God** *with all your heart and with all your soul and with all your mind." This is the first and greatest commandment. And the second is like it:* **"Love your neighbor as yourself."** Matthew 22:37–39

The first portion of this scripture, in bold type, speaks of a vertical relationship, direct with the source of life—God the Father. The second bold section is an indirect relationship with God the Father through your interaction with other people (especially your wife).

Healthy Behavior that Helps You Focus on God

1.   A daily quiet time, reading the Bible

What does this mean? You find a specific place and a specific time to be alone with God for 10–15 minutes before you start your day. During this time, you develop a relationship with him and learn to trust him. Use this time to pray, read the Bible and hear God's voice. You speak to him through prayer and he speaks to you through the Bible that you read, the feelings that you feel, and some of the circumstances during the day.

Find God in the situation; discover his will for you and your marriage.

2.   Be still and listen to God

This is good to do during your quiet time, but is not limited to that time. You can learn to listen to God at any time of the day. Learn to hear God's voice and learn to respond to it. In order to do that, you need to be quiet and attentive. In order to hear someone speak, you must be still so that you can hear. This means that the radio is off, the TV is off. The distractions of the day are distant and the focus is on God.

3.   Prayer time

This is not only done in church and on Sundays. Prayer should be a lifestyle for every day and with everyone in your family: your spouse, kids, etc. Pray with them and for them. You can pray for yourself and for others and when you do this, you are giving God the responsibility of your problems and your day. This will teach you to depend on God. This way, you will not become anxious because now your problems become God's problems.

4. Trust God in the situation

Any healthy relationship rests on trust. Trust comes by spending time together with whomever you want to start a relationship with. That is why your number one priority it to spend time with God. God loves you and wants the best for you. He also wants to spend time with you and is available to you 24/7. If you have trusted your own capability, instead of God's ability, think about how you got into the mess that you are in. Did it not happen by your own effort? What you should do is change the person you trust. Trust yourself a little less and trust God a lot more. Trusting God places the right weights into the equation. You will be surprised to discover that he is more trustworthy than you are. In order to learn to trust him, you must get to know him. See point one.

5. Memorize Bible verses

Go buy a Bible or dust the cobwebs off your existing one and commit to reading five to ten minutes a day. Bibles come in different versions. I recommend The Living Bible or New International Version translations or The Message paraphrase. You can find one in your church or on the internet. The reason you need to memorize verses is because they are the tools in your toolbox to help you grow and learn how to respond to life's circumstances. This will help your spiritual growth like nothing else will. Also, when you know where to find the thousands of promises that God makes to you, you will know how and when you can claim them. A good tool can be found at **MemoryVerses.org.**

6. Be the spiritual leader of your household

The family works together as a team, but the husband should always be the loving coach. It all stands or falls with him. This is not a sexist remark—it is a biblical principal. God designed it this way. God designed men—hardwired them, in fact—to be the leaders in their homes.

7. Owning your part

Realize that everything is not somebody else's fault. You must own your part of the problem. Once you realize your part and are willing to admit it, it will lead you to change for better. Owning your part may mean that you assume responsibility for some of the actions and inactions in your marriage. If you fail to admit that any part of the problem is yours, you will stagnate and not grow. The starting point to resolving any problem lies in recognizing where the problem is, its nature, and its source.

8. A humble attitude

Be teachable and ready to admit your mistakes and then learn from them. Humility is a desirable quality, a magnet to people. It is a virtue that is a key for change, growth, and focus on God, because he honors humble people.

9. Ask and give forgiveness

This was one of the most difficult parts for me. I could not forgive my wife even though I thought that I wanted to forgive her. I needed to understand the process of forgiveness and I also needed to understand that I could not give that which I did not have. I needed to feel forgiven in order to forgive her. Where are you with this? If you forgive, you can get on with your life. If you do not forgive, you will get stuck, become resentful or bitter and block God's blessings for you and the people around you.

10. Accountability with godly men

This comes from your support group or Bible study group or neighbors and will help you stay on the right track. You must make sure that these men who will hold you accountable for the focus on God are steadfast followers of Jesus Christ who are involved in their local church and have a healthy marriage themselves. Without accountability, we tend to go back to our old and unhealthy ways that lead to pain and destruction. Transparency and honesty are keys to growth. Integrity is what should be the hallmark of any mature man.

11. Attending church and Bible study

Find a Christian church in your area where you can connect with other Christian men through a Bible study group or a support group. **PurposeDrivenChurch.com** can give you a list of churches in your area. When you surround yourself with godly people, it helps you stay on track.

12. Service to others

Serving others helps you get the focus off yourself and onto others in a healthy manner. It makes you kind of god-like because that's what he does. He serves, loves, and doesn't care about what others think. He freely gives his time and efforts to others. Serve a cause greater than yourself.

Find serving opportunities at your local church, shelter, or any non-profit organization in your area.

13. Journal your feelings

This will help you see God's hand in your life. Be sure to write down your thoughts, your prayers, and note the ones God answered. **ChatWithGod.org** is a great resource for prayer journals. You can download one free. Or go to **FireproofMyMarriage.com**.

14. Surrender to God's plan

Surrendering to God's plan means that you accept God's will and the earthly circumstances around you as a tool to make you a more mature person. God's plan for you is that you grow in maturity, developing what is called "the fruit of the Spirit" by learning from your mistakes and developing your character. The flavors of the fruit are love, joy, peace, patience, kindness, goodness, faithfulness, gentleness, and self-control. This is the character of God in us, which we need to tap into.

How well do you apply these 14 ways to focus on God in a healthy way? Time to get started!

POINT TO PONDER

Find God in the situation; discover his will
for you and your marriage.

Are you surrendered to God's plan for marriage?

_____

_____

_____

CHAPTER 8

THE NARROW ROAD

The Narrow Road

The following graph shows the pathway of life with its unhealthy distractions and consequences (isolation, selfishness, disconnection, little growth, addictive lifestyle). These are temporary things that keep you from focusing on God. If you choose to take the narrow road, the end result will lead to a purpose-filled life for God. Jesus said in Matthew 7:13–14, *Enter through the narrow gate. For wide is the gate and broad is the road that leads to destruction, and many enter through it. But small is the gate and narrow the road that leads to life, and only a few find it.*

When you get on the road of life, as we all do, there are going to be inevitable hurdles. These hurdles or crises can be your wife threatening to leave, has already left, or is having an affair. These bumps can be conflicts with your spouse and they do hurt. It can mean pain caused by something said, something done, or something left unsaid or undone. When this happens, you will always have a choice as to your reaction. You do not choose your challenges or the way people will hurt you but you do have control over your reaction to those offenses. For sanity and healthy relationships' sake, you must learn to detach yourself from your natural response, because it will lead to further pain. Natural responses are usually unhealthy and don't lead to any healthy or spiritual growth. We call them "unhealthy cycles." Think about an offense that your spouse has committed against you that lead to a crisis. Now think about the cause. Did you do or fail to do anything that could have pushed her to do what she did?

Denial Causes the Cycle of Depression.

The typical response to a severe offense is denial. When we deny, we pretend that the offense never occurred or deny that it was offensive or even hurtful. The tendency is, however, to disconnect from the offensive

A Purposeful Life

SPIRITUAL MATURITY
HUMILITY
FORGIVENESS
UNDERSTANDING
COURAGE
TEACHABLE SPIRIT
BROKENNESS

Hope

Character

Forgiveness

Unforgiveness

ESCAPE

FEAR

SEX   ALCOHOL
CYCLE OF
DRUGS ADDICTION PRESCRIPTION
       (NO GROWTH)   DRUGS
WORKAHOLIC CONTROLLING

ME,
ME,
ME
CYCLE OF
BITTERNESS
(NO GROWTH)
                RESENTMENT
SELFISHNESS

Perseveranc

DENIAL

Suffering

RAGE
SHOCK
HURT
ANGER
PANIC
FRUSTRATION

DENIAL

CYCLE OF
ISOLATION DEPRESSION
           (NO GROWTH)
                DISCONNECTION
DEPRESSION

The
Wide
Road

CRISIS

party and withdraw emotionally. Men usually build a "wall" around themselves in order to protect themselves and keep the other one out. This isolation leads to loneliness and eventually to depression. We will call this the cycle of depression: you're not going anywhere and you're not solving anything. Find out what led to the offense. You must own whatever part is yours that caused the crisis.

> **You must own whatever part is yours that caused the crisis.**

Now think about your reaction. Did you deny, withdraw, isolate? Have you felt depressed over it? If you have answered "yes" to any of the above questions, you need to get off that cycle and get back on the narrow road. This will require persistence and denying yourself. You put aside how you feel emotionally and focus on connecting with your mate through healthy and positive communication. The way to do this is to express your indignation, but without hurting or getting out of control. Place blame appropriately. Go to the person who has offended you and let them know how you feel about what they did. The focus must not be on expressing disdain towards what was done, but towards how it made you feel. Express your desire to overcome this feeling by sharing it with the offender, if possible. What you need here is an extra dose of persistence, or perseverance. Even if you don't feel like doing this, you must keep at it because it will protect you from depression.

As you live on the narrow road, you will become more Christ-like.

Escape causes the Cycle of Addiction.

Another way we respond to an offense is by escaping. We run away, usually out of fear or insecurity. We are afraid that the offense might occur again (because we don't understand it, due to the fact that we don't want to face it, and therefore cannot prevent it from happening again). Because it hurts and is unexplainable and often unbearable, we medicate our pain with unhealthy habits that can become (denied) addictions. Rather than resolving the issue, we perpetuate the pain and repeat it in our lives. These medications can be sex, pornography, drugs, alcohol, work, or other unhealthy behavior such as controlling, explosive, and irate responses. This will lead to a cycle that we will call the cycle of addiction. Not only is it of no growth, but this one is also physically, emotionally, and spiritually destructive to self and to the relationship. What you need here is an extra dose of character. You must learn to show self control, because it is the only thing that will shield you from addictions.

Unforgiveness Causes the Cycle of Bitterness.

One of the worst ways to react on an offense is by refusing to forgive. There are two reasons we usually refuse to forgive:

1. **We don't know how to forgive.**

2. **We focus on ourselves rather than focusing on God.**

The danger caused by lack of forgiveness is that it alienates us from God as well as from the people we love the most. We push them away. When we do not understand the offense, the once natural anger response becomes stronger and stronger, instead of becoming weaker. If we do not control our anger, it will control us. The result is that we become resentful against God and/or the offender and grow bitter by seeking revenge instead of forgiving. This leads to a cycle that we will call the cycle of bitterness. The problem with it is that it defiles you and the people around you. Bitterness is like a cancer that starts small and eats you from the inside out. What you need here is an extra dose of hope. You must learn to understand the hope you have in the One who has forgiven you (Christ). This will help you stay on the narrow road and out of the cycle of bitterness.

> *Focus on God, no matter what the rest of the world is doing.*

Look at this verse and how it relates to the three natural responses by answering (denial vs. perseverance, escape vs. character and unforgiveness vs. hope): *Not only so, but we also rejoice in our sufferings, because we know that suffering produces perseverance [to keep you out of depression]; perseverance, character [to protect you from addictions]; and character, hope [to know why you should always forgive]* (Romans 5:3–4).

Once you develop these persistent traits of character and hope, you will realize that change happened because there was a certain level of surrender in you. You decided to "die to self" in order to rescue the relationship with your spouse and with God. You are allowing the Spirit of God to work in you (surrender to God) and through you (obedience to God). As you live on the narrow road, you will become more Christ-like and start developing traits that are necessary for a purposeful life. Here's what the Bible has to say about each of the positive character traits that lead to health and growth.

The *Life Application Bible* notes, published by Tyndale House, explain some of the characteristics we strive to attain.

Brokenness: Well known British evangelist, pastor, and author Alan Redpath said, "God will never plant the seed of his life upon the soil of a hard, unbroken spirit. He will only plant that seed where the conviction of his Spirit has brought brokenness, where the soil has been watered with the tears of repentance as well as the tears of joy."

> *God is more concerned with our character than our comfort.*

Praise be to the God...of all comfort, who comforts us in all our troubles. 2 Corinthians 1:3–4

Since my people are crushed, I am crushed; I mourn, and horror grips me. Jeremiah 8:21

Teachable Spirit: If you don't want to learn, years of schooling will teach you very little. But if you want to be taught, there is no end to what you can learn. This includes being willing to accept discipline and correction and to learn from the wisdom of others. A person who refuses constructive criticism has a problem with pride. Such a person is unlikely to learn.

If you love learning, you love the discipline that goes with it—how shortsighted to refuse correction! Proverbs 12:1 (MSG)

Teach me, O Lord, to follow your decrees; then I will keep them to the end. Give me understanding, and I will keep your law and obey it with all my heart. Direct me in the path of your commands, for there I find delight. Turn my heart toward your statutes and not toward selfish gain. Psalm 119:33–36

Courage: Many times, Jesus told his disciples to take courage. In spite of the inevitable struggles they would face, they would not be alone. Jesus does not abandon us to our struggles either. If we remember that the ultimate victory has already been won, we can claim the peace of Christ in the most troublesome times.

God didn't give us a cowardly spirit but a spirit of power, love, and good judgment. 2 Timothy 1:7 (GW)

Consider it pure joy, my brothers, whenever you face trials of many kinds, because you know that the testing of your faith develops perseverance. Perseverance must finish its work so that you may be mature and complete, not lacking anything. James 1:2–4

Understanding: Sometimes we feel as if we don't understand ourselves—what we want, how we feel, what's wrong with us, or what we should do about it. But God's understanding has no limit, and therefore he understands us fully. If you feel troubled and don't understand yourself, remember that God understands you perfectly. Take your mind off yourself and focus it on God. Strive to become more and more like him. The more you learn about God and his ways, the better you will understand yourself and your wife.

*Great is our Lord and mighty in power; his understanding
has no limit.* Psalm 147:5

*Husbands, in a similar way, live with your wives with understanding
since they are weaker than you are. Honor your wives as those who
share God's life-giving kindness so that nothing will interfere with
your prayers.* 1 Peter 3:7 (GW)

Forgiveness: Forgiveness involves both attitudes and actions. If you find it difficult to feel forgiving toward someone who has hurt you, try responding with kind actions. If appropriate, tell this person that you would like to heal your relationship. Lend a helping hand. Send him or her a gift. Smile. Many times you will discover that right actions lead to right feelings.

*In prayer there is a connection between what God does and what you
do. You can't get forgiveness from God, for instance, without also
forgiving others. If you refuse to do your part, you cut yourself off
from God's part.* Matthew 6:14–15 (MSG)

*And when you stand praying, if you hold anything against anyone,
forgive him, so that your Father in heaven may forgive you your sins.*
Mark 11:25

Humility: Carrying your worries, stresses, and daily struggles by yourself shows that you have not trusted God fully with your life. It takes humility, however, to recognize that God cares, to admit your need, and to let others in God's family help you. Sometimes we think that struggles caused by our own sin and foolishness are not God's concern. But when we turn to God in repentance, he will bear the weight even of those struggles. Letting God have your anxieties calls for action, not passivity. Don't submit to circumstances, but to the Lord who controls circumstances.

God opposes the proud but gives grace to the humble. James 4:6

Humble yourselves, therefore, under God's mighty hand, that he may lift you up in due time. Cast all your anxiety on him because he cares for you. 1 Peter 5:6–7

Spiritual Maturity: In the Bible, the word "perfect" means mature or complete, not flawless. God wants to see each believer mature spiritually. Like the apostle Paul, we must work wholeheartedly like an athlete or a soldier but we should not strive in our own strength alone. We have the power of God's Spirit working in us. We can learn and grow daily, motivated by love, and not by fear or pride, knowing that God gives the energy to become mature.

My friends, be glad, even if you have a lot of trouble. You know that you learn to endure by having your faith tested. But you must learn to endure everything, so that you will be completely mature and not lacking in anything. James 1:2–4 (CEV)

Therefore, as God's chosen people, holy and dearly loved, clothe yourselves with compassion, kindness, humility, gentleness and patience. Colossians 3:12

Did You Expect a Fair Deal?

If you are like most men, your answer is "yes." But a fair deal in life is not what God has promised to mankind.

This is actually God's will for you: a Christ-like character of love, joy, peace, patience toward others. How does God teach us these traits? He places us in uncomfortable or painful situations in which we are tempted to express exactly the opposite of the trait he wants to develop in us. Let me give you two examples:

1. If God wishes to develop the virtue of forgiveness in us, he will place us in a situation that will hurt us to some degree so that we will learn to forgive the person who offended us.

2. If God wants to teach us the virtue of patience, he will place us in a situation where we will have no choice but to wait, even when we don't feel like it. Our goal in any crisis or painful situation should be to relax and recognize that everything is in God's hands—both the crisis as well as the outcome.

In the midst of my crisis, I had to focus on what God wanted me to learn. I had to discover how I could grow. It's amazing how the choice to adopt God's perspective makes all those "other things" secondary and seems less important. I began to see that I really had no control over most of what happened in my life anyway. So I was more relaxed, less stressed because I had my priorities right and I was focusing on God.

...as you search to understand what is happening around you, know that bad things happen to good people.

That might seem hard to do at first or when mudslinging is going on and your life is crazy and out of control, but gradually, as you begin to let God be God, life gets, if not easier, at least less stressful. The little things in life won't hurt as deeply. They won't bother you as much as they have in the past because when you start to focus on God, all the little puzzle pieces of your life will gradually start to fit, little by little. I encourage you to do your part: learn to be proactive with God and he will direct your path. This requires you to focus on him and nobody else. Memorize this verse and pray it often:

And we know that in all things God works for the good of those who love him, who have been called according to his purpose.
Romans 8:28

As you seek to understand what God is doing in and around you, be aware that bad things happen to good people. God never promised that we would live problem free. Even though we are not going to have our way very often, be encouraged because God allows your suffering to serve a greater cause than your own. See what Romans 5:3–4 says about our suffering: *Rejoice in our sufferings, because we know that suffering produces perseverance; perseverance, character; and character, hope.*

PRAY: **Lord, remind me to focus on you. Place on my heart the areas of my character that I need to work on. Show me how I can grow through this process and teach me to embrace pain and make it my friend, knowing that you have suffered even more than I am suffering right now and that through my pain I am growing to become like your Son, Jesus. Help me to grow into the godly man you want me to be.**

It's natural for us to want to control the crises in our lives, to play God with our circumstances and with others. One way or another, you will learn there is really only one thing we have control over and that is how we react or respond to the various life situations we encounter. Let go of the false belief that you are or that you ever have been in control. Admit it and let God be God.

If you make it your goal to focus on God and allow him to control and change you, your wife, and your circumstances, you will be amazed at what he does. Your job is to respond to your wife as Christ would. Your focus should be on God and not on your wife's shortcomings.

Your obedience should be to him. Seek to understand before being understood and refrain from judging others. This honors God and he will bless you for it.

Beware of any hidden agendas or schemes on your part to control or manipulate your wife.

> **Beware of any hidden agendas or schemes on your part to control or manipulate your wife.**

No matter what is going on, ask yourself the following powerful questions: What is your motive for what you are doing? What do you need to confess? Is there an underlying issue or a hidden agenda?

When you are interacting with your wife, go for pure motives in the situation. I encourage you to talk to other godly men, reviewing your actions and plans, checking for impure motives which may be harming your marriage and corrupting your own heart. Pray for pure motives, sincere intentions in any interaction you have with your wife, and that you will grow through the situation.

Baby Steps

So here is what can you do to start making better decisions:

1. Focus on God.

2. Change the way you think.

3. Stay on the narrow road (persevere, develop character, and let God give you hope).

It's not about starting tomorrow—it's about starting to change today. It's about taking baby steps…two forward, one back, two forward, and one back. Yes, it's slow, but it is still progress. As a good counselor friend of mine, Scott Meacham, MABS, MA, PSYD (ABD), says: "It's not about perfection, it's about progress." Unless you are being proactive, it's likely you are stagnating. And, if you are stagnating, guess what? You are actually moving backwards. Don't wait until tomorrow, start today, no matter what's going on. Today is the day to make a difference, starting with baby steps, and little by little you'll make a difference for tomorrow.

"It's not about perfection, it's about progress."

Practical baby step suggestions:
- Let go and let God
- Show kindness to others
- Plan and implement a daily quiet time
- Read God-inspired books
- Help someone
- Learn to listen
- Be patient with others

"Life is like riding a bicycle. To keep your balance you must keep moving."
—Albert Einstein

PRAY: *Lord, soften my heart. Open my ears to hear you and my eyes to see you. Draw me closer to you each and every day and let me feel your presence. Light up my darkness, allow me to know that you are real and in my life today and purify my intentions. Press on the heart of my loved ones. I pray for their well being and for them to also get to know you. Amen.*

POINT TO PONDER

It's not about perfection... it's about progress

What can you do today to stay on the narrow road?

_____

_____

_____

CHAPTER 9

SO WHO ARE YOU?

When you begin examining your life closely, you may be surprised to learn that you have several hidden agendas. Maybe you are trying to control your wife, your kids, or others. Perhaps you are trying to over-protect them from their own life responsibilities. Or you might be reacting in an angry and ungodly manner in order to control a situation or a problem. Here is what you need to learn about the issues: God is responsible for the protection and the control, as well as the outcome. It's not your job, it's God's job.

> *You may be surprised to learn that you have*
> *several hidden agendas.*

What are Your True Motives?

When you start asking yourself hard questions about the events that have transpired, you may realize that your motives were, in fact, decidedly selfish and not godly at all. You may discover that you have played a major role in one or more hurtful situations. You may even find that everything may *not* be someone else's fault. It's been said that wisdom is seeing, understanding, and applying godly knowledge to life. As you seek God's help in your life, you can expect to grow in his wisdom. He has promised that. Proverbs 1:1–4 tells us, *These are the wise sayings of Solomon, David's son, Israel's king—Written down so we'll know how to live well and right, to understand what life means and where it's going; A manual for living, for learning what's right and just and fair; To teach the inexperienced the ropes and give our young people a grasp on reality* (MSG).

> *You may realize that your motives were, in fact,*
> *decidedly selfish and not godly at all.*

When the pain becomes so great that you can't take it anymore, you are finally ready to own your part. It's not solely her fault, right? Are you ready to admit that you have played an important role in the issues before you and that your motives were selfish? If so, then you can finally begin to grow.

> **When the pain becomes too great that you can't take it anymore, you are finally ready to own your part.**

You will start to grow when you are honest and transparent with everyone around you, including God and yourself. If you can admit where you have gone wrong, then it is time to ask God for help. Pray: "Lord, I need help. I need to know where I can get help in my community." Ask God to direct you to a Christian church, support group, men's Bible study group, or a Christian counselor in your community.

This is where the growth begins—on the "edge of the cliff" where you have nowhere else to turn or hide. When you are looking down and realize you have no other options, it's time to look up. Look up to God and he can finally begin to heal you. This is where God allows you to rise above the mudslinging and the ungodliness and begin to see him in your everyday life.

Today I am an entirely different person from the man I used to be when I was hurting. Back then, it hurt to be around families who were laughing. I resented the joy in their hearts. I felt that I was missing something, that there had to be more to life. Then I made a personal choice, to accept God's presence in my life, to work on myself, to stop blaming others, and to choose to live life God's way. I had to agree with the friend who said, "Lord, I'm as dumb as a rock. Gently show me the way to heal and grow."

I encourage you to stop whatever you are doing this moment—and pray. To pray means to talk to God, and to listen to God. You may feel uncomfortable or awkward at first as you wait to hear what God is saying to you. Most likely you will not hear an audible voice. But just wait and listen. Let him speak to your heart. God often speaks to us by putting impressions in our heart or thoughts in our mind.

And what does the LORD require of you? To act justly and to love mercy and to walk humbly with your God. Micah 6:8

Motives are born in your heart. Unfortunately, the heart is deceitful and can lead you to sin. Jeremiah 17:9 reminds us, *The heart is deceitful above all things and beyond cure. Who can understand it?*

The Solution: Discover God's Purposes for You

When you put God first, everything else will fall into place. You will start to think straight and you will be able to act accordingly. Jesus said in Matthew 6:33, *The thing you should want most is God's kingdom and doing what God wants. Then all these other things you need will be given to you* (NCV).

You need to know what you are all about. If you don't know who you are and what you are about, others will decide it for you. You must ask yourself who or what is currently influencing your character and your life decisions. What is the basis of your decision making? Is God in that equation? The world around you does influence you—it impacts your thinking and your choices, daily. The shifting values of our society will try to influence you, usually in a negative way. That's why you *must* know the purpose for which you were created and what you stand for. What you stand for will define who you truly are.

> *Know that the world around you daily impacts your thinking and your decision making.*

Ask Yourself: Why on Earth am I Here?

I challenge you to pray that you may learn about God's purpose for you. Ask God why he created you. When you make this your goal, you're on your way to healthy reasoning and you begin learning God's purpose for your life. Again, I encourage you to read *The Purpose Driven Life* by Dr. Rick Warren (Zondervan). You can learn the easy way or the hard way... and one of the first things to realize is that there are no accidents in life. God designed it all. Colossians 1:16 says, *For everything, absolutely everything, above and below, visible and invisible, rank after rank after rank of angels—everything got started in him and finds its purpose in him* (MSG).

God's desire is for us to grow up into the men he created us to be. It begins at birth and continues throughout our lives: it's a process. The season you are in right now is part of that process.

You can learn the easy way or the hard way...and one of the first things to know is that there are no accidents.

God refines you in the midst of your crisis. *See, I have refined you, though not as silver; I have tested you in the furnace of affliction,* says Isaiah 48:10. He reworks the rough edges and polishes off your shortcomings and your dysfunctions through pain, so that you can be used for his glory in a future season. God never wastes a hurt and he does not waste your pain. If your heart and your mind are open to what he is about in your life, you will soon discover that there are no accidents. Our lives are part of a grand design. This season may be the worst of times for you and how you feel but it can also be the best of times if you use it to draw closer to God.

This season may be the worst of times for you and how you feel but it can also become the best of times if you use it to draw closer to God.

God is in the miracle business. He reaches down into the muck and yuck—the shortcomings, the dysfunctions, and the ugliness of your life. If you seek him while you are in pain, you will find him and he will heal you and help you grow. You will be able to see him, see your part in the problems and see what he wants you to learn. Then, you will begin to discover the purpose for this season and for your life.

Life is a process and we are all in the middle of the process.

If you meet someone who professes that they have it all together, that they have nothing to learn, that there are no areas in their life God needs to work on, run and don't look back. Life is a process and we are all in the middle of that process. No one has it all together. God is in the business of reconciling all things to himself. He is also in the business of making you look more like his Son, Jesus Christ. That process is called sanctification. In that process, God allows good and bad things to happen to you—including suffering—so that you become stronger. God does this because he loves you.

God never wastes a hurt and he does not waste your pain.

Romans 5:3–5 tells us, *Not only so, but we also rejoice in our sufferings, because we know that suffering produces perseverance; perseverance, character; and character, hope. And hope does not disappoint us, because God has poured out his love into our hearts by the Holy Spirit, whom he has given us.* I encourage you not to waste this valuable season, because it teaches you how to understand God's love for you and how he won't waste a hurt, pain, or fear.

Choose: Humility or Pride?

James 4:6 says, *God opposes the proud but gives grace to the humble.* Why is being humble such a big deal to God? In my pain, I knew I had issues deep inside—underlying issues, which may very well have been the root of my relational issues. I was reluctant to face them, like my pride and self-centeredness. I needed those areas to be corrected by God. In fact, I continue to need that correction. Pride and self-centeredness are at the core of most human relational problems. For us to be able to relate in a godly way, we need Gods' presence in our life to be real. We must learn to focus on God and live closer to him.

Results of Humility:	Results of Pride:	Biblical Truth:
Leads to wisdom	Leads to disgrace	Proverbs 11:2
Takes advice	Produces quarrels	Proverbs 13:10
Leads to honor		Proverbs 15:33
	Leads to punishment	Proverbs 16:5
	Leads to destruction	Proverbs 16:18
Ends in honor	Ends in downfall	Proverbs 18:12
Brings one to honor	Brings one low	Proverbs 29:23

PRAY: *Lord, give me a heart focused on you. Give me an attitude of humility and justice so that there will be no hindrance to hear you better and know you more. Lord, allow me to put on my childlike ears and eyes to come closer to you.*

Has your heart become hardened to people and circumstances around you? Do you find yourself feeling indifferent or even inflexible toward the significant others in your life? The path that creates the distance between you and God begins with pride. It all starts with the thought that you don't need God and that you can take care of yourself, by yourself. It broadens with the failure to spend time seeking God, neglecting his will, the Bible, or other opportunities to learn about God. It reaches its apex in the way you treat your wife, children, and others. Nothing pleases God more than a life lived humbly. Simply put, the path away from humility begins with the false belief that you don't need God.

The path away from humility begins with the belief that you don't need God.

I have heard that one definition of "humility" is "the absence of any feelings of being better than others." The Bible agrees: *Be completely humble and gentle; be patient, bearing with one another in love* (Ephesians 4:2).

Examples of lack of humility:
- Pride
- Busyness
- Arrogance
- Self-centeredness
- Intolerance towards others
- Focus on self rather than on God
- A controlling behavior
- Critical of others

> *Do nothing out of selfish ambition or vain conceit, but in humility consider others better than yourselves. Each of you should look not only to your own interests, but also to the interests of others. Your attitude should be the same as that of Christ Jesus.*
> Philippians 2:3–5

If you are gifted or talented in any area of life (a skill, knowledge, or wisdom, etc.), you must be humble and grateful about it, so that God will bless you and use your talents to bless others. That's what being humble is all about: finding ways to love your neighbor with the talents God has given you. No matter how you look at it, the talents belong to God and so does your neighbor. God says, *for all souls are mine to judge—fathers and sons alike,* says Ezekiel 18:4 (TLB).

Traits of humility:

*   Consider others better than yourself
*   Model a Christ-like behavior
*   Honor and trust God
*   Overlook an offense
*   Be peaceful or a peacemaker
*   Servant/selfless attitude
*   Be childlike (not childish)
*   Be patient, gentle, and kind
*   Pray for those who have hurt you
*   Recognize your mistakes

He [Christ] must increase, but I must decrease, says John 3:30 (NASB). In today's society, humility is the anti-message, but it's the message Jesus wants us to learn. Without humility, our marriage and relationships are doomed. At some point, we all need to get this lesson: the more gifted I am in an area of life, the more humble I need to be. Even the apostle Paul, a superstar of the early church, was humbled by what he called a thorn in his flesh (2 Corinthians 12:7) because he realized that God would be made strong in his weakness.

Maybe you are especially bright or gifted. If you are, that's great. But you must understand that you have nothing that you didn't get from God— so if anyone is to be given the credit for your success, it's God, not you. Look what Jesus' brother wrote: *But whatever is good and perfect comes to us from God* (James 1:17 TLB). Thank God everyday for what he's given you, and don't take credit for it yourself. Here's why: to show off and presume is not attractive to anyone and it is inappropriate.

> **We all have shortcomings, character flaws that only God can heal.**

We all have shortcomings, character flaws, and deceitful hearts that only God can heal. But you must first admit that you don't have it all together. You must lay your problems at the foot of the cross, surrendering your issues and shortcomings to God. How do you do this? You must begin a relationship with God. It's called being "born again." Nothing else will do. This really has to be your starting point towards a new life, a new beginning. That's the starting point to the solution for your life.

PRAY: *God, I recognize that I have not lived my life for you up until now. I have been living for myself and that is wrong. I need you in my life; I want you in my life. I acknowledge the completed work of your Son Jesus Christ in giving his life for me on the cross at Calvary and I long to receive the forgiveness you have made freely available to me through this sacrifice. Come into my life now, Lord. Take up residence in my heart and be my King, my Lord, and my Savior. From this day forward, I will no longer be controlled by sin or the desire to please myself, but I will follow you all the days of my life. Those days are in your hands. I ask this in Jesus' precious and holy name. Amen.*

If you decided to pray this prayer and receive Christ today, welcome to God's family. As a way to grow closer to God, the Bible tells us to follow up on our commitment.

POINT TO PONDER

Growth begins right on the edge of the cliff, where you have nowhere else to turn or hide.

Have you secured your identity in Jesus Christ?

_____

_____

_____

CHAPTER 10

THE KEYS TO GROWTH

A To-Do List to Help You Grow

- **A daily quiet time** - Give God your day at the start of each day. It doesn't have to take long (5 to 15 minutes), but start developing a "quiet time" habit. Sit with God and offer him your day. Establish your day with God and he will establish you. This will keep your focus on God during the day, instead of focusing on yourself or your problems.

> *Establish your day with God and he will establish you.*

- **Memorize Scriptures** - Pick a short verse and learn it by heart. It will marinate in your heart if you imprint it on your mind. For example: *Be joyful always; pray continually; give thanks in all circumstances, for this is God's will for you in Christ Jesus* (1 Thessalonians 5:16–18). It can even be a portion of that verse. Memory verses will become tools in your toolbox so that whenever you need a promise from God, you will have it in your mind and you will benefit from the power of Scripture. There are thousands of promises available to you. You will only be able to claim them if you know where they are in the Bible and memorize some of them.

- **"Hang out" with godly men** - Seek out the company of Christian men. The influence of godly men will change your thinking and they will hold you accountable for your behavior. It's important to have at least one other man in your life who will hold your feet to the fire if you begin to stray. That person will also affirm you when you are on the right path.

- **Attend a weekly men's Bible study** - Find one in your area. Consult your church directory or ask a Christian friend where he goes to study God's Word.

- **Pray continually** - Develop a regular habit of conversational prayer. Give your daily problems and you marital problems to God. Prayer is your conversation with God.

- **Commit to volunteering at your local church** - Find a way to serve a cause that is greater than yourself. Church is a good place to do that. Giving back by serving others takes the focus off yourself and your problems and gives you the opportunity to put your talents to work for that greater cause. It also pleases God as you allow him to use you.

Are You Connected to the One True Vine?

Did you pray to get connected? If you did, you need to stay connected in order to be fruitful in your life. Jesus said it is the only way to be productive in life. *I am the vine; you are the branches. If a man remains in me and I in him, he will bear much fruit; apart from me you can do nothing* (John 15:5). There are two ways to stay connected to the vine:

1. **Directly connecting with God the Father** - Called "fellowship" (always through Jesus, the Son), it's accomplished by prayer, meditation, and scripture reading. This is one way that God connects with his children. Whatever you ask, you should ask in the name of Jesus, who intercedes for you in heaven and gives the power of the Holy Spirit to achieve. The sole factor of mentioning the name of Jesus invites God on board your endeavor so that you get a supernatural strength you would otherwise not have. The apostle John recorded Jesus' own words in John 15:16: *You did not choose me, but I chose you and appointed you to go and bear fruit—fruit that will last. Then the Father will give you whatever you ask in my name.* You must however be careful and not misinterpret this passage. Does it just mean saying, "In Jesus' name," at the end of every prayer, like we write, "Sincerely," at the end of every letter? No. That's not it. For one thing, if that is all it means to us, then the holy name of Jesus becomes nothing but vain repetition. It's thinking if we say the right words at the end of the prayer our prayer will be answered. There are no recorded prayers in the Bible that end with this phrase. We pray in Jesus' name because it glorifies the Father.

2. **Indirectly, by hanging out with God's family** (small groups, hanging out with other Christian people or getting involved in a Bible study or support group with other Christian men) - These two ways have

something in common: fellowship. You need it with God and you need it with his family, the church, in order to stay spiritually healthy. How do you get there? You do it by spending time in God's Word and with his people. You allow God's agenda to transform your heart.

The Transformation of the Heart

If you want to be spiritually healthy, you need to change two things: your **heart** and your **mind**. In order to do this, you need to trust in your creator, God.

Don't worry about anything; instead, pray about everything.
Tell God what you need and thank him for all he has done. Then
you will experience God's peace, which exceeds anything we can
understand. His peace will guard your **hearts** *and* **minds** *as you*
live in Christ Jesus. Philippians 4:6–7 (NLT)

God's peace will protect your mind and heart from repeating your past patterns. The transformation of your heart and mind are necessary components to a changed and blessed life. How's your heart? How's your behavior?

You know well enough from your own experience that there are some
acts of so-called freedom that destroy freedom. Offer yourselves to sin,
for instance and it's your last free act. But offer yourselves to the ways
of God and the freedom never quits. All your lives you've let sin tell
you what to do. But thank God you've started listening to a new
master, one whose commands set you free to live openly in his freedom!
Romans 6:16–18 (MSG)

You must begin to listen to God's commands and let go of your sinful life. This will start to change the way you think. Paul says it this way in Romans 12:2: *Do not conform yourselves to the standards of this world, but let God transform you inwardly by a complete change of your mind. Then you will be able to know the will of God* (TEV). A transformed heart is one that's been changed from the inside out.

Let's look at some of the aspects of a transformed heart. What does a transformed heart really look like and what does it do?

A transformed heart is:

1. **Sold out to God** - Defined as very loving or loyal. Synonyms include: faithful, true, steadfast, committed, dedicated, sold out, loving, and caring.

To be devoted is not spending time in front of a candle in a relegated cave in some distant mountain. It is an intentional and obedient action towards God and towards other people. If you made a decision for Christ, you are now a part of his family, a "saint." You are a person God chose to be part of his holy family long before the creation of planet earth. You do not behave in a godly (holy) way in order to be saved. You are saved by God's grace through faith. And because you are saved, you desire to be "holy" and behave accordingly. What does a holy life look like? Read it in Colossians 3:12–14: *So, chosen by God for this new life of love, dress in the wardrobe God picked out for you: compassion, kindness, humility, quiet strength, discipline. Be even-tempered, content with second place, quick to forgive an offense. Forgive as quickly and completely as the Master forgave you. And regardless of what else you put on, wear love. It's your basic, all-purpose garment. Never be without it* (MSG). "Holy" means chosen, set apart, having a special purpose.

> A transformed heart is one that's been changed from the inside out.

2. **Committed to God** - Are you sold out to God, fully surrendered concerning your time, your resources, and your mind? *Jesus replied: "Love the Lord your God with all your heart and with all your soul and with all your mind and with all your strength"* (Mark 12:30). This is the first and greatest commandment.

3. **Dedicated to be the best for God** - Is being the man God made you to be the primary desire of your heart? *In a word, what I'm saying is, Grow up. You're kingdom subjects. Now live like it. Live out your God-created identity. Live generously and graciously toward others, the way God lives toward you* (Matthew 5:48 MSG).

4. **Humble towards God and his people** - If people could see inside your heart, would they find love and humility there? *For whoever exalts himself will be humbled and whoever humbles himself will be exalted* (Matthew 23:12).

5. **A praying heart** - Are you giving God your problems regularly and not holding them back? *Pray continually* (1 Thessalonians 5:17).

6. **A grateful heart** - *Give thanks in all circumstances, for this is God's will for you in Christ Jesus* (1 Thessalonians 5:18).

7.   Surrendered to God - Give him everything you've been struggling to hold on to—your wife, your anxieties, and your problems. *Surrender to God! Resist the devil and he will run from you* (James 4:7 CEV).

8.   Stays close to the source - If you prayed to accept Christ as your Lord and Savior, then you can rest assured that he will never leave you and you will never lose what you have gained. *Remain in me and I will remain in you* (John 15:4).

> *Do you seek instant gratification instead of trusting in God for the provisions you need? This is where most of your havoc comes from.*

9.   Does God's will - When others look at you, do they see a man who reflects godly character in all his thoughts, words, and actions? What directs your path? *Do not merely listen to the word and so deceive yourselves. Do what it says* (James 1:22).

10. Learns to obey God and commits to grow - Are you quick to obey, no matter what God asks of you, or do you resist if it's too uncomfortable or difficult? *The person who continues to study God's perfect teachings that make people free and who remains committed to them will be blessed. People like that don't merely listen and forget; they actually do what God's teachings say* (James 1:25 GW).

11. Learns to love God as well as ungodly people - The transformed heart is capable of distinguishing between the sinner and the sin. We must learn to love people, no matter what their sinful condition is and we must do so without condoning their sinful behavior. If another person you know is caught in a sin, you must help that person in a loving way, Galatians 6:1 says, *Brothers, if someone is caught in a sin, you who are spiritual should restore him gently.* Again, the binding virtue is love. Love is the only godly strength available to you that empowers you to forgive the sin unconditionally. *Above all, love each other deeply, because love covers over a multitude of sins* (1 Peter 4:8).

12. Focused on eternity - Do you seek instant gratification and not trust in God for the provisions that you need? This is where most of your havoc comes from—your unwillingness to trust that God will meet all of your needs. *And my God will meet all your needs according to his glorious riches in Christ Jesus,* says Philippians 4:19. It's not natural for men to believe that which cannot be seen. Scripture tells us to focus our eyes on things above. *So we fix our eyes not on what is seen, but on what is unseen. For what is seen is temporary, but what is unseen is eternal,* 2 Corinthians 4:18 tells us. Jesus is seated at the right hand of God, interceding for you and all your needs. Colossians 3:1–2 says, *Since, then, you have been raised with Christ, set your hearts on things above, where Christ is seated at the right hand of God. Set your minds on things above, not on earthly things.*

Fruit of the Spirit

When you become a new you, a new creation, something internal happens that will have external and eternal implications. It's the fruit of the Spirit. In order for you to live according to God's precepts, you need God's support. Part of this support system will be found in his Spirit and in the fellowship of his people. If you are connected to the vine, you will produce fruit in your character, which we call the fruit of the spirit. It consists of nine flavors, as described in the book of Galatians.

> *But the Spirit produces love, joy, peace, patience, kindness, goodness, faithfulness, humility and self-control.*
> Galatians 5:22–23 (TEV)

Notice that it starts with "love." Love is the first flavor (fruit) of the spirit because love is preeminent. *Meanwhile these three remain: faith, hope and love; and the greatest of these is love* (1 Corinthians 13:13 TEV). Love is also the greatest commandment: *Jesus answered, "Love the Lord your God with all your heart, with all your soul and with all your mind. This is the greatest and the most important commandment. The second most important commandment is like it: "Love your neighbor as you love yourself"* (Matthew 22:37–39 TEV).

1.   **LOVE:** This is the virtue that binds it all together. If you have true, godly love, the rest of the flavors (fruit of the spirit), will also be present in your life. If you miss the mark of love, you will miss it with peace. You'll also miss it with joy, with patience, and all the other flavors. You must start with love and therefore, you must start with God, because love is the essence of God.

2.   **JOY:** If you love your wife as you are supposed to love her *as Christ loved the church and gave his life for her* (Ephesians 5:25), it will be natural for you to enjoy life with her. Conversely, if you do NOT love your wife in the

way that you are supposed to, you will NOT experience the joy of life with her (nor will she with you).

3. PEACE: If you love your wife as you are supposed to love her, it will be natural for you to live peacefully with her. Conversely, if you do NOT love your wife in the way that you are supposed to, you will NOT experience peace when you are with her (nor will she with you).

4. PATIENCE: If you love your wife as you are supposed to love her, it will be natural for you to be patient with her. Conversely, if you do NOT love your wife in the way that you are supposed to, you will NOT display patience towards her (nor will she towards you) but you *will* be quick to anger (and so will she).

5. KINDNESS: Titus 3:4 tells us that Jesus is "the kindness of God." If you want to know what kindness is, just look at Jesus and allow his spirit to inhabit your heart. John 13:15 says, *I've given you an example that you should follow* (GW). God never asks you to do anything for anybody else that he hasn't already done for you himself. If you love your wife as you are supposed to love her (as Christ loved the church and gave his life for her), it will be natural for you to be kind towards her and her feelings. Conversely, if you do NOT love your wife in the way that you are supposed to, you will NOT be kind to her (nor will she to you).

6. GOODNESS: If you have the love of Christ in you, you will also have his goodness and it will be natural for you to be good to your spouse. If your desire to be good to your wife is not present in your heart, you might not be close to the source that will give you that goodness.

7. FAITHFULNESS: God does not intend faithfulness in marriage to be boring, lifeless, pleasureless, and dull. Sex is a gift God gives to married people for their mutual enjoyment. Real happiness comes when we decide to find pleasure in the relationship God has given or will give us and to commit ourselves to making it pleasurable for our spouse. The real danger is in doubting that God knows and cares for us. We then may resent his timing and carelessly pursue sexual pleasure without his blessing. God calls us to be faithful and joyful.

8. GENTLENESS: Gentleness is often overlooked as a personal trait in our society. Power and assertiveness gain more respect, even though no one likes to be bullied. Gentleness is love in action—being considerate, meeting the needs of others, allowing time for the other person to talk, and being willing to learn. It is an essential trait for both men and women. Maintain a gentle attitude in your relationships with others.

9. SELF CONTROL: Many religious people say that self-control is not needed because "deeds" do not help the believer anyway (2 Peter 2:19). It is true that deeds cannot save us, but it is absolutely false to think they are unimportant. We are saved so that we can grow to resemble Christ and so that we can serve others. God wants to produce his character in us. But to do this, he demands our discipline and effort. As we obey Christ, who guides us by his Spirit, we will develop self-control with respect to our emotions and relationships.

Our faith must go beyond what we believe; it must become a dynamic part of all we do, resulting in good fruit and spiritual maturity. Salvation does not depend on good deeds, but it results in good deeds. A person who claims to be saved while remaining unchanged does not understand faith or what God has done for him or her.

By the way, this application of love and other flavors of the fruit of the spirit is true for the husband, just as it is for the wife. The fruit of the spirit is the reflection of Jesus living inside of us, no matter if you are a man or a woman. A true convert to Christianity will display this fruit as he/she grows. The amount of fruit produced will also increase through time, as the disciple (you) develops a Christ-like character.

POINT TO PONDER

A transformed heart is one that's been changed from the inside out.

Are you connected to the one true vine?

_____

_____

_____

CHAPTER 11

SHE'S THE ONE HAVING AN AFFAIR

What to do?

Wisdom is the ability to view things God's way and apply them according to his will. There is no doubt that the world offers you an incredible amount of distractions to keep you from focusing on what is right, pure, or excellent. What is right? What is wrong? Can you tell the difference? If you can, it will be easier for you to stay focused and not get distracted by worldly stuff, which will lead to mudslinging, focusing on self, among other unhealthy distractions. Although what is distracting you may be healthy, it may lead to a reaction that is unhealthy. Just as there are things you do that are not necessarily bad…they are simply not necessary. Some of these distractions may be fun and entertaining or even stress relieving, but the time spent in the distraction could be time spent nurturing the marriage.

Is Your Wife Having an Affair?

If she is, the issue is not the affair. The issues are why it happened and how you respond to it. A man we will call Joe came to one of our meetings. This is his story:

"She was the perfect woman for me," Joe told the group one night. "From the first time we met back in college, she had been the most trusting, loving, and fun woman I knew. I trusted my life to her. All of my friends and family loved her and were overjoyed when I announced she had accepted my wedding proposal and would soon become my wife. She was incredibly giving and loved to cook and take care of people and she loved doing all the same things I had a passion for. We enjoyed traveling together. We both had great jobs and it seemed like everything we did together turned out perfect. She even had the same weird sense of humor I had and to me, no one understood or cared about me more than she did. I felt the same way about her. She was the only woman I had ever been intimate with. In my eyes, she was the most beautiful woman in the world, my best friend, and life partner. We were perfectly matched, perfectly compatible. She was perfect—I thought. Or was she? Now, I understand that nobody is perfect and I mistakenly put her on a pedestal where she didn't belong (nobody belongs on a pedestal, except for God)."

"Then one night I came home from work late to find a phone conversation that had been mistakenly recorded on our answering machine. It told me she had been having an affair with her boss for more than a year. My whole world caved in."

What do you do if your wife is having an affair? The following statement may be difficult to hear and even harder to understand, but it's true nevertheless: This is God's problem, not yours.

That does not mean that you become complacent or indifferent about it. It means that you must become proactive and cooperate with God to understand, forgive, and grow out of this situation.

If your wife is having an affair...what is your part?

Joe went on. "She immediately moved out, once she became aware I had finally found out. I was totally numb, traumatized, and in shock. I couldn't believe this was happening to me. I shouted why, why? What had I done to deserve this? How could she? The one that I was faithful to for all those years…for nothing? How could she throw all that away? What a lack of respect and consideration towards my faithfulness and her own vows. What about the kids, our marriage? Does all of that go down the toilet? Is that what she wants, to throw it all away? I desperately needed to talk to someone I could trust and who could understand what I was going through, but who? I didn't have any answers to all these questions. All I could do was speculate the answers, her feelings, her motives and these speculations would only send me in a faster and deeper emotional spiral that would spin me out of control. It would generate anger and disorientation."

Joe went on: "The sleepless nights and the inability to talk with anyone I could trust had started to take a toll on me. I really needed to talk to a pastor. As I began telling him my story, all my pent up emotions unfolded. I completely lost it. I remember choking out the words, 'You don't know how I feel! You can't imagine how it feels to have your heart ripped out of you and then walk around emotionally bleeding to death while trying to put on a smiling face each day at work. Nobody I work with knows what's going on inside me!' I was a ticking time bomb of anger and rage caused by pain, fear, frustration, and confusion."

"'I know exactly how you feel,' I heard the pastor say. 'Because I also experienced what you are going through. And I'm here to tell you that if you have faith in God, he will get you through it…just like he got me through it.' Then he listened patiently as I told my story in detail, even during the times when I could barely get the words out and had to stop for several minutes at a time, because I just couldn't go on."

"More than an hour later, he gave me several verses to go home and meditate on. He said I needed to learn to live one moment at a time. Step-by-step, because that's how Jesus did it. I remember this verse that he gave me: 1 Peter 2:21 (MSG), 'This is the kind of life you've been invited into, the kind of life Christ lived. He suffered everything that came his way so you would know that it could be done and also know how to do it, step by step.' He explained that there was power in the memorization of scripture. Now I know that he was right."

"'Memorize them and count on the Lord to keep all his promises to you,' the pastor went on. 'I don't know how he's going to do it right now, Joe, but I can tell you that God will somehow bring the best out of your suffering and heartbreak. He promises that if we will trust him and keep praying and seek his will for our lives and stay focused, he will direct our path.'"

"For the first time in weeks I had some hope back in my life. Even though it appeared my marriage and 'dream life' were both over, I could at least begin walking down the long road that would ultimately lead to my emotional recovery."

We question what we should do in a major crisis. If your wife is having an affair, it is a major problem in your eyes and certainly in God's eyes. What is your part in the affair? "My part?" you say. "You didn't hear me correctly. I said that it was my wife who is having the affair." As cold as it may seem, if your wife is having an affair or if you believe she may have a relationship outside your marriage, I'm asking you again: what is your part? As much as it may hurt you, there is a reason why your wife is having the affair and very possibly, you are a big piece of the puzzle. We don't often do something we know is "wrong" unless we have unmet needs of some kind. Is it possible you have contributed to her infidelity by failing to meet a need or needs in her life?

> *If your wife is having an affair or if you believe she may have a relationship outside your marriage, I'm asking you gently, what is your part?*

This offense hurts incredibly and your emotions are all over the place. You are injured and profusely bleeding. What will you take care of first, the offense or the bleeding? Is she gone for good? Will you ever trust her again? What about the kids? It may be hard to explain all the emotions that you are currently feeling because they are all coming to you at the same time. Here are some examples of emotions you may be feeling: You are overwhelmed and there might be feelings of insult, shame, embarrassment, pain, rage anger, revenge, and the like. How about letting the world know what she's done? Then again, that will increase your shame. All these feelings are clouding your perspective and may misguide you as you take your next move.

What is Your Next Move?

Here are your options:

1. **Seek revenge and hurt her at least as much as she hurt you.** This would be any normal man's natural response. It's OK to feel this, but don't act on it, because although it is a natural response, it is not a healthy one. You will seek revenge, then she will seek revenge back. One or both of you end up either in the pit of despair or in jail. Seeking revenge is not a good response. It doesn't lead to where you want to go: it leads to bitterness.

2. **Pretend it didn't happen.** You can hide for awhile with drugs, work, alcohol, or other distractions, but denial is a dangerous response because it will not allow you to process the offense. It will keep you from grieving and impede you from growing. This response makes you shut down emotionally, withdraw so that you do not seek nor accept to connect with others. Denial throws you in a pit of despair and eventually… depression. Not healthy. Also, there is no real possible reconciliation without forgiveness. There can be no forgiveness if you pretend that there was no offense. You must face the truth and allow it to guide you in a constructive response.

3. Obsessing about the event. This is what we call "chasing your pain." It is another dangerous habit. If you suffer because of the offense and feel the need to explain and understand it, you will tell and retell the offense in your mind and ask questions and details about the occurrence. Unfortunately, you are not ready to process all the details nor should you, because every single additional detail makes you additionally angry and leads to more questions about more details. Don't ask detail questions. Don't do research, don't hire a private investigator, don't search the cell phone records. These all lead to more questions that you are not ready to handle. You will find all the necessary information in God's time.

4. Seek to understand and forgive. This option is very different than the previous ones. Now you try to understand the reasons for the choice that the offender made. Your focus is not on the person nor the offense, but rather the bad choice that the offender made. You intentionally avoid retelling the story in your mind so that you will not become obsessed with it. Now, you do not seek to "know the details." Instead, you make the intentional choice to place the blame appropriately and get to know the unmet needs that pushed her to choose the wrong path. That means you admit that an offense has really occurred, that it really hurts, and it is because a need was not met. This is an important step towards grieving, forgiveness, and hopefully, reconciliation. This does not mean that it is your entire fault and yours only. But it does mean that some of the blame might be yours for not meeting her needs. Your spouse might have felt that her needs had not been met and will not ever be met by you. Whether you agree or not, her feelings are real to her and she is entitled to them. Her fears, feelings of rejection, abandonment, or emotional neglect are real to her. In order to have those needs met, she searched (or is searching) for them outside of the marriage boundaries, which is clearly wrong and cannot be justified in any way. The only way that adultery can be forgiven is through God's power.

Men don't have strength, will, or understanding to forgive, except surrendered to God.

What could you have done to avoid her going outside of the marriage? How could you have met her needs? What could she have done to avoid it? What could she have done to express her needs to you? Did you not hear her? Are you able to see that you have lived a selfish life in your marriage? Know that every action has its consequences. You may be sorry for everything you may have said or done that hurt her. God will forgive you, but the consequences will still be there, so that you may learn.

5.   Pray in crisis: Prayer is man's most powerful tool, particularly in the midst of a crisis. Most of the time, you won't be able to see God in the midst of your situation, but he's there. You just can't see clearly because you are emotionally confused and disoriented because of the shock and pain. But God wants to connect with you and that is best done through prayer. You must pray from the heart, which means that you are not only praying for yourself and your situation, you also pray for others (your wife, her lover, etc.).

PRAY FOR:
*   *Wisdom and discernment.*
*   *God's will to be done.*
*   *His strength and self control.*
*   *That this situation will soften her heart and yours.*
*   *Understanding of what is happening and why.*
*   *The situation will bring you and your wife closer to God.*

Here's a different type of prayer that is intentional and altruistic. If your wife is having an affair, consider the Hedge of Thorns Prayer.

The Hedge of Thorns Prayer

This focused and intentional prayer should be used when someone we love needs a specific protection by letting God erect a wall of spiritual protection. We call it the building of a spiritual "hedge of thorns" that will keep the enemy's forces out.

In Psalm 24:3–4, we read, *Who may stand before the Lord? Only those with pure hands and hearts, who do not practice dishonesty and lying* (TLB). There are several prerequisites for this prayer to be effective:

*   You must have a clear conscience and pure motivation. This means that there is no unconfessed sin in your life and that your motivation for this prayer is for the well-being of your mate. If you are holding on to unresolved sin or resentment towards anyone, take a few moments to confess it. God tells us in his Word, *Have you not put a hedge around him and his household and everything he has?* (Job 1:10). The Hedge of Thorns Prayer is to be used when your spouse is either having an affair or behaving

inappropriately and it involves asking God to intervene in the situation. In this prayer, you are asking God to protect your wife and to change those individuals who are involved with her so that they are no longer interested in having a relationship with her. This is not to be prayed to harm anyone. It is to be prayed so that God will surround your wife with love and protection and so that she will be convicted regarding what she may be doing.

• You must have a personal relationship with God. If you're not, why put it off any longer? By now you surely see that this is the only way to a meaningful life filled with hope. Let this moment be the true beginning of new life for you, no matter what happens with your marriage. Christ will give you purpose in life and a sense of direction you've never known before. There's no magical formula—just pray something like this:

> PRAY: *Jesus Christ, I believe you are real and I want to have a relationship with you. I want you to be my savior and the Lord of my life. I'm sorry for having let you down with the life I've led up to now, but I want to turn it around if you'll help me do it. Please come into my heart right now and show me how to live my life for you.*

Note: If there is unresolved sin, anger, rage, or a hidden agenda on your part, this prayer will not be appropriate. You must have accepted Christ as your Lord and Savior, and you must surrender your situation to God 100 percent.

> PRAY: *Heavenly Father, I ask You in the name and through the blood of the Lord Jesus Christ, to build a* <u>*hedge of thorns*</u> *around my partner. I pray that through this hedge, any other lover will lose interest and depart. I base this prayer on Your Word, which commands that "what God has joined together, let man not separate."*

Some results of praying the Hedge of Thorns Prayer may include:

• Your wife may become confused and lose perspective: *Therefore I will block her path with thornbushes; I will wall her in so that she cannot find her way* (Hosea 2:6).

- Others in the relationship often lose interest: *She will chase after her lovers but not catch them; she will look for them but not find them* (Hosea 2:7a).

- Troubles may increase as God encourages your spouse to return to the marriage: *Then she will say, "I will go back to my husband as at first, for then I was better off than now"* (Hosea 2:7b).

None of this is meant to imply that you are to forget about your wife's actions or to take her back immediately. But it's a way of demonstrating that you rely on God and will let God be God in this tough situation.

In order for you to keep your sanity, you must not focus on the injury, seek revenge, or seek to judge even while you are bleeding. We are all people who make bad choices. In his *Seven Habits of Highly Effective People*, author Stephen Covey mentions that one of the "habits" is to understand before being understood. Ask yourself: What led to the bleeding…what led her to the affair? Don't judge what she did… that's not your job. I encourage you to try to understand her choice: She made a bad choice but that doesn't make her a bad person. She could be a good person making bad choices. After all, you didn't marry a bad person, right? You married a good person and if she is behaving badly now, could it be that hanging out with you turned her that way? So let's take the premise that she is a good person who made a bad choice. There will always be consequences for any bad choice in our life. If you choose to forgive, there still will be consequences. There will be consequences of what she has done and there might even be more consequences from the causes that led her to the indiscretion. The consequence is a fruit from her free will. Your free will led you to a different choice. You must choose to get on the path of forgiveness, no matter what her next step might be. I will develop the issue of forgiveness more in the second volume of this series.

> *The only way to recover from hurt is by forgiving.*

The pain you go through may have you wondering where God is in the midst of your storm. Be aware that even though you are not seeing him nor sensing his presence, just know that he is there holding you up and protecting your heart and mind (*You will keep in perfect peace him whose mind is steadfast, because he trusts in you* (Isaiah 26:3).). Keep on casting your cares to him and he will keep on guiding your steps. Be what it may, know that God is in the midst of your crisis today. You may have heard or seen this story:

FOOTPRINTS IN THE SAND

One night a man had a dream.
He dreamed he was walking along the beach with the Lord.
Across the sky flashed scenes from his life.

For each scene, he noticed two sets of footprints in the sand.
One belonged to him and the other to the Lord.
When the last scene of his life flashed before him,
he looked back at the footprints in the sand.

He noticed that many times along the path of his life,
there was only one set of footprints.
He also noticed that it happened
at the very lowest and saddest times in his life.

This really bothered him
and he questioned the Lord about it:
"Lord, you said that once I decided to follow you,
you'd walk with me all the way.
But I have noticed that during
the most troublesome times in my life
there is only one set of footprints.
I don't understand why when I needed you the most
you would leave me."

The Lord replied,
"My precious, precious child,
I love you and would never leave you.
During your times of trial and suffering,
when you see only one set of footprints,
it was when I carried you."

~Author Unknown~

God will carry you through if you let him. In order for you to benefit from God's presence during your trial, there are some things that you will need to do. You'll need to cooperate with God in forgiveness. He has forgiven you when you asked him to, but what if you had not asked him to? What if your wife does not ask for forgiveness, will you still forgive?

This is an important step, because your physical and spiritual health depend on it. If you choose not to forgive, you will either enter into a depression or bitterness. If you choose to forgive, you will release the heavy burden of bitterness and resentment, no matter whether she comes back or not.

The most important person you want around you right now is God and not your wife.

The most important person you want around you right now is God and not your wife.

God is not indifferent about your feelings. He knows and wants what is best for you. Your wife wants what she believes is best for her. Only God knows what is best for both of you.

As God begins to work on you and your heart condition, you will begin to uncover some of the missing pieces of the puzzle.

You must be honest with yourself and admit that some of this was caused by you. Therefore...own your part.

Can you do that? Can you say: "I have a part in this. It may have been my poor attitude, my work schedule, my not being emotionally present. It's possible that I abandoned my wife, emotionally and physically, that I was not a godly man in my home. I failed to share all areas of my life with my spouse and I have a major part in this ugly, horrible affair"?

You must focus on what happened in your relationship, when and over what period it happened. But most of all, you must identify your part in this situation. Once you have done this... give it to God. He will then guard your heart and your mind. That is part of his plan.

Below are some of the reasons your wife may be having a relationship outside the marriage:

- **I was emotionally distant**
- **I was not affectionate with my wife**
- **I worked too much**
- **I did not honor her**
- **I was emotionally abusive to her**
- **I was not the spiritual leader in my home**
- **I was not an example of a godly man in my home**
- **I was unfaithful**

There is no excuse for your wife's poor decision or her behavior, but you must focus on why this happened and what your part was and is for its occurrence.

> *Strive to be a godly magnet, so your wife will see God in you.*

POINT TO PONDER

If your wife is having an affair... what is your part?

What is your part in your wife's affair?

_____

_____

_____

CHAPTER 12

DO YOU DATE WHILE SEPARATED?

Flirting with the Opposite Sex While Separated

I ran across a friend sitting in church with a female who was not his wife. We will call them Jim and Betty. Jim attends one of my men's groups. He is currently separated, because his wife is having an affair with another man. Betty is also separated from her alcoholic and abusive husband. Jim is hurting because while his wife is enjoying her self-centered life and having an affair, he has been served with divorce papers from her attorney. Betty kicked her husband out, so feels free and can finally breathe.

As I observed Jim and Betty from a distance, I noticed that Jim was getting some playful attention from Betty, who although separated, is not yet divorced. It may have been an innocent outing to church or wherever else they went after church and it sure felt right for both of them at the time, but it was inappropriate and wrong.

Why you should not date while separated:

1. Both parties are emotionally empty. Both are wonderful people, but in this season, they are so hungry for attention, needy for contact, desperate for someone to talk to, and anxious for acceptance that they are too empty to be in a healthy relationship.

2. Neither of them really have anything healthy to offer to the other. Neither of them is ready to embark on a new relationship—yet.

3. They are both still legally married, though not to each other, under common law, as well as under moral law.

4. It might lead to adultery. According to the courts, they still have marital obligation to their spouses, and according to God, flirting with the opposite sex while still married is adultery. Jesus says in Matthew 5:28, *But I tell you that anyone who looks at a woman lustfully has already committed adultery with her in his heart.*

5. When we are hurt because of a betrayal, we become vulnerable to revenge and seeking a way to temporary heal our hurt with a patch or "good company." Spending time with a person of the opposite sex while you are vulnerable is asking for trouble and may lead to a compromising situation that will likely lead to more hurt.

Reality says that when you are hurt, you need healing. Spending time with another person of the opposite sex is not healing, even though it feels good. In order to heal, one must go through a grieving process. This process cannot work in the context of a distracting new relationship. On top of it all, you would now be increasing your probability of another failed relationship.

Statistics say that first-time marriages fail at a rate of approximately 50% and second- and third-time marriages fail at rates of 67% and 74%, respectively (*What to Watch for Today*, by Jay Granat, www.divorce360.com). The issue at hand is that before you embark on a new relationship, you need to be healthy first. You also need to learn from your past—and still painful—experience. Another person in your life would be a distraction and an obstacle to growth and self-evaluation. It makes sense that you want to take your time, for the sake of processing the hurt, planning the recovery, and learning to live again. If you get divorced, you should wait a minimum of one year from the time the divorce is final (not the time you were first separated) before you remarry.

Masking the pain does not lead to emotional health, healing, or recovery.

What you should do while separated:

First, you must know that in your situation, you are not alone. There are millions of broken homes, broken hearts, and broken dreams. Families are shattered and relationships become dysfunctional. Masking the pain does not lead to emotional health, healing, or recovery. It only helps you ignore the pain, camouflage and deny it. Second, you must come to grips and accept that you are in this situation for a season. That means that it is not a place to stay, but it is a place to start your healing process. It's a place of transition.

You need to unlearn old habits and learn new ones. Start to learn how to cook. Discover that you can watch a movie without missing your spouse. Start doing things by yourself, such as going to the park, reading a book, or hanging out with other reliable and trustworthy men. Spend real time with your children without your wife there having to remind you.

Understand why you are where you are, and in the meantime, love on your kids who need their daddy. Children are not responsible for what parents do, but they do feel guilty and suffer more than they should. Parents do not realize this while they are overcome by their emotional and selfish baggage. This is not the time to be selfish or self-centered. This is the time to give your time and service to others.

How to start healing while separated:

If you want to be healthy again, you must take the time to reflect, meditate, and heal. This happens best in the context of support groups or men's groups or meetings that will address the attention of your neediness. You will find it helpful to join a support group in your church, talk over your hurt and current emotional state of mind with a counselor, and discover God's will in a Bible study. I suggest all three. The Bible tells us to, *Abstain from all appearance of evil* (1 Thessalonians 5:22 KJV). Being with a person of the opposite sex may seem innocent, but it may also be a deception to lure you from doing what's right. If it is not done out of faith, then don't do it. It is said that "perception is reality." Don't put yourself in a situation that you will not want to explain to your spouse later on. It is almost guaranteed that she will find out.

You need to unlearn old habits and learn new ones.

Why you must not date while separated:

Let me say unmistakably that dating while you are still married is one of the worst possible things you could do and it is morally wrong. You are married; you have made a commitment to God and to your wife and family. That commitment is unconditional. This means that the vows that you have made are still valid and may not be broken just because you feel like knowing someone else in a more intimate way. You swore in front of God (even if you did not marry in a church) that you would love, honor, cherish, in sickness and in health, until death do us part. If you and your wife are separated, that means you are both still alive and you are legally married to one another until the divorce is pronounced final by a judge. I have seen hearts changed on the final days of a divorce proceeding because of the pro-marriage stance taken by at least one partner or third party in the process—and those marriages are together today as a family. You've got to give God the full opportunity to do his work in all the hearts involved. If you decide to date before you are biblically permitted, you are short-circuiting his plan and he will not bless your new relationship.

God wants to work in your life, in your marriage, and in other areas of your life. If you follow your fired-up emotions to get a divorce and date other women during a separation, you will impede God from working in your marriage relationship and your personal growth. Let God be God and do his work.

He loves you and wants to help you be all that you can be. He wants to redeem your relationship, your marriage. But if you step outside of his relational parameters and protection, several things you will not like are likely to happen and other things that you would like in life will not happen.

If you partially cover your eyes with your hand, you will have an incomplete view through the gaps between your fingers. If you then throw in a couple of pretend smoke bombs or a few pretend hand grenades into the mix and with all of these distractions ask yourself if you can rationally make any clear decisions about your surroundings, you will hopefully realize that you do not have the complete perspective (view) to make an informed decision. To top it off, your emotions are inciting you to be reactive instead of proactive. She may be in sin and out of line, but you must stay in line. This is for your own good and the good of your future. If you must make a decision, make sure that it is a rational one and not an emotional one. That's where you are in your state of separation—peeking through your fingers while missiles are going off around you. Emotionally, you are hurt, confused, and fearful. You are in such a state of confusion that you may not be able to make clear and rational decisions. When you make reactive decisions based on your negative emotions, instead of rationally-driven decisions based on godly principles, you are setting yourself up for failure and conflict.

Men make plans (so do women), but the outcome will always include God's desire for you to grow closer to him, have a healthy perspective of your future and a hope. The prophet Jeremiah said, *"For I know the plans I have for you,"* declares the Lord, *"plans to prosper you and not to harm you, plans to give you hope and a future"* (Jeremiah 29:11). He will not prosper you nor give you hope and a future if you stay out of his will. Dating during a separation is out of his will and not in your best interest.

Does your marriage matter to you? Despite all the wrongs, offenses, and mudslinging…don't give up. You will miss 100% of the shots that you do not take. Hang in there and focus on doing what is right. The main thing is to keep the main thing, the main thing. Ask yourself: What is the main thing to you? What is the main thing to her? You must show how important your wife is to you by your actions and how much your marriage matters to you. You do that by choosing not to date while still married. Your wife wants to feel that she's the center of your world and nothing says, "I'm over you" faster than dating somebody else.

Dating someone else during a separation is the same as having an affair and constitutes adultery. If you are considering dating somebody else in order to get back at her or because you need somebody, it is neither a valid nor a healthy reason. God will not honor any adultery and neither will your wife. Would you think that it is honorable? What is your excuse behind the desire for dating somebody else? No excuse is valid, if you are still officially married. You are rationalizing that you need to go outside of your marriage in order to fill that emptiness deep inside. The only thing that can fill that void is the love of God. It will fit perfectly. If dating someone else is a rectangle or a square and the void inside of you is a circle, it won't fit. The dating will not fill your need. If you believe that it will, you believe a lie and are being deceived.

What is the right thing to do? What is the healthy thing to do? Do you want to be emotionally healthy? Then do what's right: *don't date!*

Stop for a moment and ask yourself, "Who in their right mind would be attracted to someone who is not whole or healthy in their personal relationships?" The answer is simple. That would be someone who is also not healthy or whole and most likely very needy. Is that the kind of person you would want to date? Don't ask someone else to become involved with you during this season. Get your life straight first.

Focus on Becoming a Healthy, Whole Person

Without question, you have enough issues on which to focus during this season of life, without the added complication of a new relationship. When facing conflict, you must focus and ponder on the following three points:

- How can you grow through this conflict?
- How can you honor God in this conflict?
- What can you do to serve the other (her)?

Be certain of this: anyone who wants to date you while you are separated is not your angel from heaven.

No godly person with your best interests in mind would consider violating God's Word in this way.

During this time there are safeguards you must have in place for your own protection and one of them is to not put yourself in a one-on-one situation with someone of the opposite sex. Don't be alone together in an office, a car, or a conference room, because your vulnerability is real. Watch out for any position that potentially leaves you alone with a woman to whom you are not married or who is not your mother or sister.

Is there a woman you know who is sympathetic towards you and your situation? You may try to convince yourself that it would never happen to you, that you are only friends. Don't try to fool yourself. You will fail and that will only bring more pain between you and your wife. You are extremely weak and vulnerable right now and therefore open to unhealthy attachments. It may feel good that someone is paying attention to you and listening to your pain, but all you'll really get for the few moments of pleasure is more pain and an unnecessary delay in your healing process. You've got to learn why you are experiencing your current situation and you won't do it by getting involved with someone else. Instead, get help by sharing your pains with a support group such as a Men on the Edge ministry in a local church or a men's Bible study group or a local counselor (a man).

Be certain of this: Anyone who wants to date you while you are separated is not your angel from heaven.

POINT TO PONDER

You need to unlearn old habits and learn new ones.

Do you still believe it is acceptable to God for you to date someone else while separated?

_____

_____

_____

CHAPTER 13

LAWYERS AND MEDIATORS:

Rarely the Right Answer

Many professions have conflicts of interests in their dealings with customers. They make money while you end up picking up the tab or paying their commissions. Usually, they gladly take your money (a lot of it) while they rarely have your well-being (or your wife's) at heart. At Saddleback Church in Lake Forest, California, we prefer not to follow the route of lawyers or mediators, although sometimes they are needed to help address legal issues, such as rights infringements or custody battles, abuse, etc....

From my experience, if we respond in anger using an iron fist, we will lose the war and we will push our wives away. The softer, kinder approach goes much further at this junction in the road. I strongly encourage you not to seek out a lawyer unless you have been served. Yes, you need to know your rights, know your options and the consequences of a legal action. But far more important is this fact:

God is looking at your heart condition.

Filing for divorce or beginning any legal proceedings in that direction is NOT in your best interest, nor is it in God's plan for you. Divorce is NOT God's will for your marriage. God HATES divorce. He says, *"I hate divorce," says the Lord God,* in Malachi 2:16.

During my marital crisis, I was broke, scared, anxious, and uncertain of tomorrow. The last thing I needed was a bill from a lawyer. God provided a creative way to for me to know my legal rights, what the consequences of a divorce would be and then to only respond to the legal proceedings after I was served.

God loves you and wants to help you be all that you can be.

The consequences of a divorce will be lived, carried, and suffered by your kids, leaving years of pain and dysfunction for them. The tearing apart of your family and years of lost dreams are certainly not what's best for you or your kids and it is not what God desires. Some counselors will go as far as to convince their counselees to do what they think is best for themselves, rather than focusing on the bigger picture of life. If you are to leave a legacy behind, the first place where that will become a reality is with your offspring. Think of your own relationship to yourself, your relationship to your wife, and your relationship to your children. Then, think about God's position in each of those relationships. You do not seek legal advice lightly, for yourself only. Rather, look after the best interest of your family members. The apostle Paul mentioned it in a different context: *Each of you should look not only to your own interests, but also to the interests of others* (Philippians 2:4).

> *In God's eyes, the more we know, the more we are responsible for.*

Therefore, do not focus on the legal side of things; focus on God's command to look after one another. Do not initiate a divorce yourself; it is not in anybody's emotional nor spiritual interest. God wants us to be gentle as doves and wise as serpents. Seek to rise above the name-calling and mudslinging. Determine now to be a man of integrity when that moment comes—and then watch God come through for you.

In God's eyes, the more we know, the more we are responsible for. Jesus says in Luke 16:10, *Whoever can be trusted with very little can also be trusted with much, and whoever is dishonest with very little will also be dishonest with much.*

If you start a divorce, God could hold you more accountable for the consequences. Additionally, such actions will push your wife into the hands of attorneys—and further away from you. I always share this with men in my support groups, "Rise above the situation. Do not play dirty; rather play on God's team."

> *The tearing apart of your family and years of lost dreams are certainly not what's best for you.*

Who Wins When You Rise Above It All?

If you allow bitterness to take root in your heart, you will discover that you are holding something similar to a rattlesnake by the tail—and you may eventually get bitten. So who wins when you rise above the situation? Everyone does (except the lawyer). Your kids win, your marriage wins, and God smiles on you for being a godly man and an example to others.

> *In the same way you husbands must live with your wives with the proper understanding that they are more delicate than you. Treat them with respect, because they also will receive, together with you, God's gift of life. Do this so that nothing will interfere with your prayers.* 1 Peter 3:7 (TEV)

You're a winner every time you rise above the situation and don't engage in the mud slinging.

What the Bible Says About Divorce

There are permissible provisions for divorce, such as in Jesus' Sermon on the Mount and Paul's exhortation to the Corinthians:

> *But I tell you that anyone who divorces his wife, except for marital unfaithfulness, causes her to become an adulteress and anyone who marries the divorced woman commits adultery.*
> Matthew 5:32

> *To the married I give this command, (not I, but the Lord): A wife must not be separated from her husband. But if she does, she must remain unmarried or else be reconciled to her husband. And a husband must not divorce his wife.*
> 1 Corinthians 7:10–11

Remember that to rationalize is to tell a "rational lie." In your isolation, the advice that it's OK to leave your spouse is nothing more than a huge lie from society (lawyers make money from that lie so there might obviously be a conflict of interest). That lie is fueled by our enemy, who will do anything he can so that your actions will go against the will of God. God says: "I hate divorce." Therefore, Satan says, "go ahead and divorce."

Remember that Satan hates all mankind and will stop at nothing to see us destroyed and/or separated from God.

Since marriage is a union that symbolizes Christ and the Church, Satan hates it. Once we've become God's property, Satan will do anything he can to make our lives miserable and destroy our faith so that we will doubt God's love for us. It's what he lives for. So here's the question: are you going to let Satan win? Or are you going to let God win?

While it is true that marriage is a lot of work, your efforts will pay off dividends that will bless you, your wife, and your children.

While you try to **rationalize reasons** why you might need a lawyer, check any of the following statements that come to mind.

- ☐ "She will never change"
- ☐ "She is always angry"
- ☐ "She doesn't respect me"
- ☐ "She is an emotional rollercoaster"
- ☐ "She spends too much $$$"
- ☐ "She makes me mad"
- ☐ "She has unrealistic expectations"
- ☐ "She is high maintenance"
- ☐ "I just need to be happy"
- ☐ "It's not my fault"
- ☐ "I don't love her anymore"
- ☐ "We don't have sex often enough"

Did you notice that there is not one mention of the appropriate place of focus in any of these statements? Look again in chapters 6 and 7: Where is your focus? We must keep our focus on God and off of ourselves and off of our spouse. Ask yourself: Are you in a healthy, God-focused relationship or in an unhealthy, self-focused relationship?

The desire to divorce or to get on with something new (try to be happy) is usually a sin of choice that has become acceptable in our society.

We choose to water down the vows, rationalize our new desires, and justify why it's OK to split and divorce. But it really comes from not focusing on God.

Does this sound familiar? "I just need to be happy and move on with my life." Society sells divorce. The numbers are frightening. Research shows that a divorce costs an average of $30,000 and a court battle for child custody can cost another $15,000–$50,000 for each side (David G. Schramm, www.marriageresourcecenter.org). When you add those numbers, you will realize that divorce is not only emotionally devastating but financially as well. In 1997, the legal industry (lawyers) cashed in an estimated $34,890,000,000 (almost 35 billion dollars). This does not take into consideration the additional cost of living separately, paying for two households, and the consequential visits to psychologists, and other medical, mental, and indirectly related issues that stem from a divorce.

> *The desire to divorce or to get on with something new (try to be happy) is usually a sin of choice that has become acceptable in our society.*

Actually, a lot of people have made divorce an industry. It's been my experience that a lot of our reasons for divorce today are trumped up by unbiblical reasons. We just want our way and we want it now. We justify it with, "You don't understand how hard it is to stay in my marriage." Or: "She's doing this or she won't do that." Or: "She just won't change." Or worse: "I just need to be happy."

You are confusing "needs" with "wants."

Let's get to the nitty-gritty: it really is a spiritual problem, because you are trying to fill the circle-shaped hole with a square-shaped divorce.

Divorce is a spiritual problem, because your needs and/or her needs can ultimately only be filled by God or by a God-driven marriage.

You are confusing "needs" with "wants."

It's Between You and God

I really do understand what you're going through. I have walked your road before you walked it. It is a hard, narrow road with a lot of twists, turns, and potholes. God wants you to focus on him in the midst of your crisis. It's not about what your wife is doing. Actually, it's not about her at all: It's about you.

It's about God and you—that's the road you need to be on. Others will want to distract you and pull you in a different direction. It's been my experience that when there is a marital crisis, it is because either one or both are now unplugged from God's fellowship. Satan whispers: "It's OK, you deserve to be happy. You deserve a better life. All you have to do is walk out the door." And they listen. After all, it sounds so good and so right. The root of this problem is what needs to be addressed, rather than using a patch to feel better. The root of the problem—what got you where you are—is that you have failed to be the spiritual leader in your home. You have not led your marriage into spiritual intimacy. You have probably lived in union but not as one flesh.

So check your connections. Have you unplugged from God—and from other godly people? Have you sinned by allowing your spouse to disconnect? You see, that is your responsibility.

You may think you want to start over — try something (or someone) new.

But the grass is not greener in a new relationship. Grass is green wherever you water and fertilize your lawn.

Can The Dysfunction Brought by Divorce be Passed On to Your Children?

Without a doubt, the choices we make for ourselves will influence the lives of others, including our children. A friend of mine once asked me: "Gary, when did you learn how to drive?" My answer was that my dad wouldn't let me drive until I was almost 18. But I already knew how to drive, I told my friend, because ever since I was two years old and sitting in the backseat of my dad's station wagon, I could see his driving skills and tell myself: "Hmm, so that's how to drive – or that's how not to drive." Either way, we imitate. Things with kids are caught and not taught. They watch what we do; how we react to situations. They imitate what they saw us do. They may or may not make a conscious choice to imitate, but they follow what was patterned for them in the home. Once upon a time, you were also a kid in the backseat

The choices we make will influence the lives of others, including our children.

of life. What did you learn? It's how you are wired, and changing the programming is not easy to do. So yes, your children, also, can be dragged into your poor decisions and the ugliness of divorce. Your poor choices will not only impact their childhoods as they are caught in custody battles or shuttled between households and parents, but the emotional consequences continue to be felt many years later, in their adult life. Children of divorced parents battle becoming adults who also divorce because the pattern has been laid out for them.

If none of the above works, someone may advise you to consider mediation instead of a legal process that involves attorneys. Be careful! Mediation is often a wolf disguised in sheep's clothing. Is a mediator any different from a lawyer or an attorney? Other than the cost and the amount of time spent to come to an agreement, it is basically the same whenever the mediator pushes toward a divorce. Instead of focusing on divorce, you should focus on what God wants you to learn in your situation and how you can grow in becoming more like Christ. THAT is God's will for your life!

The Danger of Mediation

Christian mediation may help you resolve your issues without losing your wallet, your sanity or your faith—**as long as the focus is on reconciling with your spouse.** The danger of mediation however, is that it usually is a quicker and faster way to a divorce.

> *Now, for those who are married I have a command, not just a suggestion. And it is not a command from me, for this is what the Lord himself has said: A wife must not leave her husband. But if she is separated from him, let her remain single or else go back to him. And the husband must not divorce his wife.*
> 1 Corinthians 7:10–11 (TLB)

If you have ever participated in a lawsuit or survived a divorce, you are all too aware of the tremendous expense and emotional stress involved. Litigation can cost you thousands of dollars and several months, or even years of your life. Christian mediation may help as long as the focus is on reconnecting with your spouse. Additionally, the emotional and spiritual damage caused to every person involved can be irreparable.

Fortunately, you have a choice when faced with difficult issues. Some say that Christian mediation is an affordable alternative to litigation. Some even dare to say that it can allow you to take biblical control of your dispute without losing control of your finances. It may be true, but many times it is a disguise.

The Bible discourages Christians from bringing lawsuits against other Christians in secular courts of law (1 Corinthians 6:1–8), and instructs us that God desires that Christians be reconciled to one another when disputes of any nature arise between them (Matthew 5:21–24; Matthew 6:12, 14; Matthew 18:15–20).

What is Christian Mediation?

Christian mediation can be a faith-based approach for resolving disputes utilizing biblical principles, prayer, discernment, and creative problem solving, in view of reconciliation. However, this is not always the outcome. A mediator can also be an attorney disguised in mediation clothing with the same conflicts of interest as explained in the previous chapter. It is true that as Christians we are called to love one another and to make every effort to settle a dispute out of court whenever possible (Matthew 5:25–26). But we know that a mediator also needs to make a living and that living may come at the detriment of the reconciliation of your marriage. I believe we should seek to reconcile, because that is the task we receive from God:

> *All this is from God, who reconciled us to himself through Christ*
> *and gave us the ministry of reconciliation: that God was reconciling*
> *the world to himself in Christ, not counting men's sins against them.*
> *And he has committed to us the message of reconciliation.*
> 2 Corinthians 5:18–19

POINT TO PONDER

You need to unlearn old habits and learn new ones.

Are you confusing "needs" with "wants"?

_____

_____

_____

CHAPTER 14

HOW TO RESOLVE ISSUES BIBLICALLY

In order to live the life that you were meant to live during this difficult moment in your life, you will have to reframe your thinking, feeling, and acting within these parameters:

1. **Focus on God**

2. **Learn to forgive**

3. **Whenever possible...reconcile the relationship**

Christian mediation may help you resolve your issues without losing your wallet, your sanity or your faith, as long as the focus is on reconciling with your spouse. But if it becomes a fast track to divorce, it is not God's will for your marriage.

What is God's will for your marriage?

☐ Divorce   ☐ Reconciliation   ☐ Litigation

Share your response with a friend who will hold you accountable for your decisions.

Look up 1 Corinthians 6:1–8, Matthew 5:21–24, and Matthew 18:15–20.

Forgive us our debts, as we also have forgiven our debtors.
Matthew 6:12

For if you forgive men when they sin against you, your heavenly Father will also forgive you. Matthew 6:14

RECONCILIATION IS NOT A QUICK FIX

What would you do if your mediator or your lawyer is still leaning towards a divorce but you know that God's will is to see you and your wife reconciled?

Somewhere deep inside, you know that a quick-fix will not solve your issues, it will not develop your character and will only draw you further away from realizing what was once a dream. Here are two verses to consider:

Not only so, but we also glory in our sufferings, because we know that suffering produces perseverance; perseverance, character; and character, hope. Romans 5:3–4 (TNIV)

Careful planning puts you ahead in the long run; hurry and scurry puts you further behind. Proverbs 21:5 (MSG)

One of the virtues that gets too little attention these days is persistence—perseverance over time in pursuit of a noble and worthwhile goal.

It is interesting to me that in the verse just cited, the Bible places "perseverance" midway between "suffering" and "character." There's just no shortcut from one to the other.

If you really want to develop your character, stick to the marriage, make it work. And if you really want to stick to the marriage, develop your character to be more Christ-like.

Do all you can to forgive and/or be forgiven and reconcile, if possible. But don't expect it to be a "quick fix."

> **If you really want to develop your character, stick to the marriage, make it work. And if you really want to stick to the marriage, develop your character to be more Christ-like.**

In order to forgive, all you need is an internal decision that you can make on your own. But in order to reconcile, you need to know the heart of the person you wish to reconcile with. It might be that the other is unwilling to reconcile, in which case reconciliation is not possible.

Forgiveness is a command, while reconciliation is an option. However, if you wish to reconcile, you must forgive first and commit to continue to forgive on a regular basis. Once reconciliation has become a possible option, the path to learn to trust again is once more open.

> **Be proactive with God and with your wife as you lead the family back together.**

How to Initiate Reconciliation

Couples who are looking for reconciliation in their relationship should consider the following steps:

1. Think about specific attitudes and behaviors you are doing that contribute to the conflict. *Your attitude should be the same as that of Christ Jesus* (Philippians 2:5). He was humble of heart and spirit.

2. Admit those attitudes and actions to your spouse at an appropriate time and pray. This is not a talk you want to have when you are tired, hungry, or indisposed in any way. *Therefore confess your sins to each other and pray for each other so that you may be healed. The prayer of a righteous man is powerful and effective,* says James 5:16.

3. Now, apologize. The twelve most important words in marriage are "I was wrong. I am sorry. Please forgive me. I love you." It is impossible to have a healthy relationship with God, while holding grudges against people. Matthew 5:23–24 says, *This is how I want you to conduct yourself in these matters. If you enter your place of worship and, about to make an offering, you suddenly remember a grudge a friend has against you, abandon your offering, leave immediately, go to this friend and make things right. Then and only then, come back and work things out with God* (MSG).

4. Search for creative solutions that will improve your relationship. We generally try to solve the problems before we fully understand them—we get the tip of the iceberg and run with it. Try hard to understand and meet your wife's needs (the bottom of the iceberg). At this point, listening becomes more important than speaking. Listen until each person feels understood. By doing this you stand a much greater chance of solving the problem and moving on. Philippians 2:3–4 says, *Do nothing out of selfish ambition or vain conceit, but in humility consider others better than yourselves. Each of you should look not only to your own interests, but also to the interests of others.*

In order for a marriage to work you must communicate. You have to talk about the little things that may seem trivial (like leaving your socks on the floor, the toilet seat up instead of down, and which way you squeeze the toothpaste tube), so the little things don't become big things. You need to be wise in choosing which battles are worth fighting. You can win small battles while losing the war.

Plan the Reconciliation

Before you even consider going back home, it's important to have a written plan of reconciliation, and then to have it reviewed by your pastor, counselor, joint or individual counselors, and trusted godly accountability men around you. Ask them to look for flaws in this joint plan. Be proactive with God and with your wife as you lead the family back together.

Depending on your situation, this is likely to be an extremely delicate operation. No matter what your relationship was like in the past, or what may have caused the separation, the reconciliation will work best if done on mutual terms. If she is requesting that you move back into the home, it's critical that you, your pastor, and/or your Christian counselor agree that this move is best for all parties. The plan must be clear and agreed upon.

Be proactive with God and with your wife as you lead the family back together.

Go to **www.MenOnTheEdge.com** to find a reconciliation checklist.

Having your reconciliation plan written in detail, signed, dated, and reviewed by both parties helps you stay on target and in line with what a godly marriage is intended to be. You are also showing your wife how important she is to you, and how important your marriage is to you.

If you plan for success, you will have a greater chance of succeeding in your reconciliation. You may have ups and downs in the implementation of your plan, and you may have to adjust the plan from time to time, and that's OK. Strive for clarity in your plan, have accountability for both parties written into your plan. Find other healthy and mature couples you can model your marriage after and with whom you meet with occasionally to stay on track. Attend marriage seminars whenever possible to encourage and review what a godly marriage is and how your marriage can be improved.

Even as you move forward, be aware that setbacks are normal. Strong forms of accountability enmeshed in your reconciliation plan help keep your marriage on track. I encourage you to not return to your old character behaviors or bad habits that may have contributed to your original marriage problems. Make it your goal to continue communicating with your wife, feeling her frustrations, empathizing with her emotions, and focusing on being emotionally present one day at a time. With a positive attitude and with God at the helm you will succeed.

> *With a positive attitude and with God at the helm*
> *you will succeed.*

How Big is Your God?

When you pray and trust God, wait patiently. Anything is possible. Trust God. He will not let you down. Give your marriage to God. Give him your finances, your job, and your relationships. Once you've given it all to him, your job should be to submit to his plan, whatever that may be. You must learn to do what the Bible commands and let him work out the circumstances. Then, you must get out of the control-game that you are sabotaging yourself in. The false sense of control that you have been enjoying is a lie that you have been led to believe. Another lie is that you need to control the people around you in order to be happy. When you let God be God, you are actually getting out of God's way and letting him control your life and do his work.

> *Consider the influence God may want you to be in the lives*
> *of those you love.*

If you allow God to be God, he will help you through this situation. If in your mind God is too small to help you, or you might think that your situation is too small for God, then it won't work. God really cares for all his children. All their problems are known to him and he cares about it all. That's how big God is. That is also the size that you must reflect when you are dealing with others. Allow other people—even your enemies—to see the greatness of God. You might just be that one person who helps your friend, neighbor, or family member hear God's truth in a loving way.

I have big issues with the credibility of self-help authors. The first problem with self-help is in the first word: "self." We were created by God to have a life of fellowship with him and not with self. The second issue that I have with these self-proclaimed authors is that they are merely authors of books. Nothing tells me that they have actually lived out the same problems that I am facing. If I want to learn something from someone, I am going to find an expert in the matter, someone who has walked the path of pain. Most "self-help" TV programs done by celebrities are simply money-making minutes designed by actors for the cause of entertainment or stimulation, but little of it is useful.

God, on the other hand, has suffered a great divorce. Our relationship with him started with a divorce in the Garden of Eden. His church, whom we represent, keeps on falling and disappointing him, yet he continues to come to the rescue, forgiving and redeeming his flock. That's the kind of leader that I need to follow and emulate. That's greatness. But the actors and talk show hosts are entertainers. Where are they in the midst of your pain? How do they live? How much pain have they caused, versus the pain of others they might have helped alleviate? They may want to hide their poor lifestyle and poor choices by being a TV "authority," while what they're really doing is masquerading their true face and distorting the truth as written in God's Word.

If you allow God to be God, he will help you through this situation.

Think about that for a while and consider the influence God may want you to be in the lives of those you love… Consider that their choices are constantly being slammed by a world that is constantly lying to them and really doesn't care about them.

Consider the influence God may want you to be in the lives of those you love.

Staying Under God's Umbrella

When you stick to the marriage in the way that God has designed it, you pray for God's words, wisdom, and discernment and you reflect God's love in all your relationships. That is how you live God's plan for you and your family.

God's Word is our umbrella, protecting us from the consequences of unnecessary storms.

The flip side is when we are outside of God's umbrella and outside of his protection. We are trying to live life on our own power. We are trying to reinvent God's original design. Outside God's umbrella, we only get drenched. Under God's umbrella, there is peace. Listen to what he himself has to say about it in Psalm 19:7–11:

The law of the Lord is perfect, reviving the soul.
The statutes of the Lord are trustworthy, making wise the simple.
The precepts of the Lord are right, giving joy to the heart.

The commands of the Lord are radiant, giving light to the eyes.
The fear of the Lord is pure, enduring forever.
The ordinances of the Lord are sure and altogether righteous.
They are more precious than gold, than much pure gold;
They are sweeter than honey, than honey from the comb.
By them is your servant warned;
in keeping them there is great reward.

Do you beat yourself up? I know I did and I imagine most of us do, whenever we live outside of God's umbrella. So, what value is there in doing that? Learn from your mistakes and only look back for learning purposes. Beating yourself up for a past you cannot change doesn't make sense for a future you only desire. Ask for forgiveness for your past and move forward. Live proactively, with God leading the charge.

> **Learn from your mistakes and only**
> **look back for learning purposes.**
> **Ask for forgiveness for your past and move forward.**

POINT TO PONDER

With a positive attitude and with God at the helm,
you will succeed.

Where can you allow God to be God and help you with your problems?

_____

_____

_____

CHAPTER 15

YOUR ANGER AND YOU

Our goal in this chapter on anger is to help you understand the nature of anger, how to deal with it in a healthy and mature way as you work toward rebuilding your life, and growing stronger in Christ. The key is Christ. If he is constantly at the center of your life—your thoughts, your decisions, your actions, and your anger, you will become the man he has designed you to be.

Many churches have been telling their members that anger is evil and therefore sinful. There are obviously verses that would support this theory in the New Testament as well as the Old Testament. Jesus himself, in the Sermon on the Mount, said, *But I tell you that anyone who is angry with his brother will be subject to judgment* (Matthew 5:22). And Proverbs 29:22 tells us, *An angry man stirs up dissension and a hot-tempered one commits many sins.* On the other hand, two people got angry in the Bible without sinning. Do you know who they are?

1. God himself. In the Old Testament there are 375 times that God got angry. So being angry is a natural and God-given emotion.

2. The other person who got angry, without sinning, is Jesus. Matthew 21:12 says, *Jesus entered the temple area and drove out all who were buying and selling there. He overturned the tables of the money changers and the benches of those selling doves.* He also displayed anger towards the Pharisees in Mark 3:5: *He looked around at them in anger.* So we know that if Jesus got angry on several occasions and so did God the Father, we can rest assured that expressing anger (without sinning) is possible and permissible.

Unfortunately, the way in which we express anger many times leads to sin because we allow anger to escalate to fury and rage, which can be hurtful to our relationships and even to our own health. Anger will adversely change your thinking capacity and obscure the clarity of your thinking process. Most of the biblical heroes have shown anger at some point in their lives and some of them did it with serious consequences, because their anger obstructed their clear thinking. This is where it is appropriate to remember this verse: *In your anger do not sin: Do not let the sun go down while you are still angry* (Ephesians 4:26).

Wrong display of anger

Moses, the leader that God himself handpicked to lead his people out of bondage in Egypt, grew angry at the people of Israel, and in his anger sinned by disobeying God. When the Israelites were complaining that they had no water to drink while in the desert, God had ordered Moses to "speak to the rock." Numbers 20:8 says, *Take the staff and you and your brother Aaron gather the assembly together.* **Speak** *to that rock before their eyes and it will pour out its water. You will bring water out of the rock for the community so they and their livestock can drink.* Moses was so angry at the bickering and whining from the people and their lack of faith in God that he himself disobeyed God and **struck** the rock, instead of speaking to it, as clearly ordered by God. The consequence of his disobedience cost Moses the fulfillment of his dream: he would NOT step foot in the Promised Land because of his mistake. Numbers 20:10–12 says, *[Moses] and Aaron gathered the assembly together in front of the rock and Moses said to them, "Listen, you rebels, must we bring you water out of this rock?" Then Moses raised his arm and struck the rock twice with his staff. Water gushed out and the community and their livestock drank. But the Lord said to Moses and Aaron, "Because you did not trust in me enough to honor me as holy in the sight of the Israelites, you will not bring this community into the land I give them."*

Right display of anger

The challenge is to be angry for the right reasons, at the right time, with the right person, and expressed in the right way. The Bible says in Ephesians 4:26, *In your anger, don't sin.* Anger can be harmful, but anger can also be helpful. Sometimes, anger is even necessary in order to grieve and forgive. The difficulty is to control anger. When you are able to control your anger, it becomes a virtue known as meekness, or strength under control. Meekness is important to acquire because it reflects the character of Christ. It is one of the flavors from the fruit of the Spirit. Galatians 6:1 says, *Brothers, if anyone is caught in any transgression, you who are spiritual should restore him in a spirit of gentleness. Keep watch on yourself, lest you too be tempted* (ESV).

The issue today is not how you should get rid of all your anger, but how can you express your anger in a godly (positive) way? Here's what Rick Warren says:

Rick Warren on "Anger"

There are four ways people commonly express their anger. I call it the M & M's of anger or the 4M's. These are learned responses. Everybody expresses anger in the way they learned to express it. Some of you learned it from your parents, some of you from television, from friends, or from your wife. You've learned how you respond. I once heard the four expressions of anger described using these picturesque words: 1. the Maniac; 2. the Mute; 3. the Martyr; and 4. the Manipulator.

1. The Maniac - This guy is so explosive, his nickname should be TNT. Anything could set him off and usually does. When he loses it, don't be in the way. Watch out for the overspray of toxic words and rash actions. Cain in the book of Genesis could be seen as the original Maniac (Genesis 4:5,8).

Once the Maniac has spent his ammunition, he is usually sorry for what he did. He immediately regrets his anger and may even be embarrassed by his actions—but he can't take them back. He wishes it hasn't happened, but the damage is done. Ever seen anyone like this? I have. We all have.

2. The Mute - The Maniac's polar opposite is the Mute—the silent type. Whatever he's feeling he stuffs down inside. He clams up instead of blowing up. If you ask him how he's feeling, he'll deny any anger that may be bubbling below the surface.

One person called this "the crock pot version of anger—stewing and simmering and it's all on the inside." Biblically, the Mute is exemplified in Jeremiah, the weeping prophet (Jeremiah 15:17–18). Silent anger isn't really hidden forever. It manifests itself often in physical illness, as the Mute's feelings eat him alive.

3. The Martyr - This guy is a real party animal—if you like pity parties. No one beats him at accepting blame or taking on guilt. When you look up the word "depression" in the dictionary, his picture is there. "What's wrong with me?" he asks. "Why am I always messing up?" His vocabulary is laced with words like "I should...must...have to...ought to..." Like the Mute, the Martyr's depression is usually covering up un-vented anger. Remember the Lost Son's older brother? He is a classic picture of the Martyr (Luke 15:28). The Martyr is known for deflating everyone's balloons.

4. The Manipulator - This is the guy who smiles at you and congratulates you on your promotion, while figuring out how to one-up you behind your back. Church people often choose this person as it is a less obvious type of anger. Pleasant while you're in the room, but before you walk out—make sure the rest of the crowd has their umbrellas. The Manipulator pretends to be nice, but really just wants to get even.

The Pharisees were great Manipulators. Consider this description of them in Luke 6:11: *But they were furious and began to plot with each other what they might do to Jesus.* Let's face it: we all get angry. It's just that it doesn't always look the same, which makes it easier to pretend we really weren't ticked off. Be honest with yourself.

As you read the descriptions, which one described you? The good news is that all four types are learned, which means they can all be unlearned. By recognizing your anger type, with God's help, you can change your life."

So what is your anger style?

☐ Maniac

☐ Mute

☐ Martyr

☐ Manipulator

Who did you learn your anger from?

☐ Dad

☐ Mom

☐ Siblings

☐ Work Buddies?

How can you defuse your anger?

Some say that anger is a secondary emotion, usually triggered by a primary one such as frustration, confusion, insecurity, pain, fear, or a combination thereof. One way to take the "grrr" out of your anger is by looking to God, instead of others or self. Your self worth (insecurities) also plays an important role in this emotion. Understanding your value in God's eyes is essential to assuring your identity and therefore essential in controlling you anger. Self-secure people do get angry but express it appropriately while insecure people are easily angered for almost no reason at all and burst out of control.

> *The more insecure you are, the more you'll depend on the opinions of others to feel good about yourself.*

In Ecclesiastes 7:21, Solomon cautions us, *Do not pay attention to every word people say.* The more insecure you are, the more you'll depend on the opinions of others to feel good about yourself.

So if someone puts you down, you're going to be hurt or get angry and want to fight back. The secret to overcoming anger is to let your self-image be who Christ says you are. When you are confident in Christ, it doesn't matter what other people say about you. If someone puts you down, you can ignore it. It just doesn't matter because you know it isn't true.

Finding your value in Christ helps you handle hurt, frustration and insecurity without endangering others.

He who fears the Lord has a secure fortress, says Proverbs 14:26. If God likes me and I like me, then if you don't like me, you've got a problem. When I realize that, I'm not so angry. When I feel positive about myself fewer things are going to threaten me, frustrate me, or hurt me. You have to learn to accept what God says about you. God says you're OK. He has a purpose for your life. Then you're not so uptight over what other people say about you, and your anger level goes down.

Five verses on anger to memorize

Verses like these will help you express your anger adequately:

> *He who guards his lips guards his life, but he who speaks rashly will come to ruin.* Proverbs 13:3

> *Pride only breeds quarrels, but wisdom is found in those who take advice.* Proverbs 13:10

> *A gentle answer turns away wrath, but a harsh word stirs up anger.* Proverbs 15:1

*The tongue of the wise commends knowledge, but the mouth of the
fool gushes folly.* Proverbs 15:2

*A hot-tempered man stirs up dissension, but a patient man
calms a quarrel.* Proverbs 15:18

PRAY: **Lord, give me the strength to recognize my anger and to
deal with my anger in a meek fashion. Help me realize how
inappropriately I am reacting at times and to know that with your
help, Lord, I can grow to be more and more like you.**

As I look in the mirror, what do I see?

- ☐ A person I don't like?

- ☐ An angry man who is quick-tongued?

- ☐ A poor listener?

- ☐ A poor spiritual leader?

- ☐ A workaholic?

- ☐ A man with a poor attitude?

Anger is a signal—and it's one worth listening to.

I realize it's been all too easy for me to point the blame at others, saying, "It's not my fault, it's her fault."

Perhaps there is a wounded little boy inside who wants out, wants to grow up, who longs to grow into a godly man.

*"For I know the plans I have for you," declares the Lord, "plans to
prosper you and not to harm you, plans to give you hope and a future.
Then you will call upon me and come pray to me and I will listen to you."*
Jeremiah 29:11–12

The Blessings of Anger

From *The Dance of Anger: A Woman's Guide to Changing the Patterns of Intimate Relationships,* by Harriet Goldhor Lerner (Harper Paperbacks 1997).

Anger is a signal—and it's one worth listening to. Our anger may be a message that we are being hurt, that our rights are being violated, that our needs or wants are not being adequately met or simply that something is not right. Our anger may tell us that we are not addressing an important emotional issue in our lives or that too much of our self— our beliefs, values, desires, or ambitions—is being compromised in a relationship. Our anger may warn us that others are doing too much for us, at the expense of our own competence and growth. Just as physical pain tells us to take our hand off the stove, the pain of our anger preserves the very integrity of our self. Our anger can motivate us to say "no" to the ways in which we are defined by others and "yes" to the dictates of our inner self.

POINT TO PONDER

The more insecure you are, the more you'll depend on the opinions of others to feel good about yourself.

How can you use your pain for the good of everyone involved?

_____

_____

_____

CHAPTER 16

HOW TO CONTROL YOUR ANGER

What is Anger and How Can We Control It?

There is no doubt that anger is responsible for a lot of damage in our world. But God says there is a place for anger. In fact, anger is a God-given emotion. The Bible has a lot to say about anger and how to express it. Here are just some examples:

In your anger do not sin. Do not let the sun go down while you are still angry. Ephesians 4:26

Make no friendship with an angry man and with a furious man do not go. Proverbs 22:24 (NKJV)

The north wind brings forth rain and a backbiting tongue an angry countenance. Proverbs 25:23 (NKJV)

An angry man stirs up strife and a furious man abounds in transgression. Proverbs 29:22 (NKJV)

For as churning the milk produces butter, and as twisting the nose produces blood, so stirring up anger produces strife. Proverbs 30:33

But I say to you that whoever is angry with his brother without a cause shall be in danger of the judgment. And whoever says to his brother, "Raca" shall be in danger of the council. But whoever says, "You fool" shall be in danger of hell fire. Matthew 5:22 (NKJV)

Let all bitterness, wrath, anger, clamor and evil speaking be put away from you, with all malice. Ephesians 4:31 (NKJV)

But now you yourselves are to put off all these: anger, wrath, malice, blasphemy, filthy language out of your mouth. Colossians 3:8 (NKJV)

Anger is an energy that offers tremendous constructive potential when it is controlled and put in action creatively. It is like nuclear energy; like dynamite. The bad news is that anger energy is also tough to control. Therefore, it needs to be wisely used. The good news is that anger is learned—it is not inherited. An angry temperament can be altered with practice and prayer.

Here are some other things you should know about anger:

- Anger is an automatic response to hurt, frustration, or fear.

- Anger is physiological arousal—nothing more.

- Anger signs: a stimulus (externally or internally) triggers emotion, tension begins to build, adrenaline is released, breathing rate increases, heart beats faster, blood pressure rises, eyes opens wider, we lose control of our thoughts.

- Anger is simply a state of physical readiness. When we are angry, we are prepared to act and respond to our hurts, frustrations, and fear.

What is aggression?

Anger and aggression are significantly different.

- Aggression is the violent expression of anger.

- Aggression always hurts somebody.

Most of us handle our anger poorly, making tense situations worse.

God gave us the gift of becoming angry. If we did not get angry, we would be defenseless when we are faced with hurt, frustration, or fear. When we are angry we have enormous power available within us. What we choose to do with that anger can move us like a missile to a place of resolution and peace, or to a point of devastation and destruction. Everyone expresses anger differently, but the patterns are always predictable. Most of us handle our anger poorly, making tense situations worse. We end up driving our point away from our goal rather than getting where we need to get.

Anger is an energy that offers tremendous constructive potential when it is controlled and put in action creatively.

Anger is an energy that offers tremendous potential when it is controlled.

How Can you Tame Your Words and Your Actions?

If out of control anger has been an issue for you, the good news is there are several techniques to help you regain control and defuse inappropriate anger. One that works really well is keeping a written track of your anger.

Keep a simple anger journal. Get to know yourself by getting in touch with your feelings. What hurts you, frustrates you, saddens you? What are you afraid of? What makes you happy? Pray every day and ask God to help you before you start writing.

> *Complain if you must, but don't lash out. Keep your mouth shut,*
> *and let your heart do the talking. Build your case before God*
> *and wait for his verdict.* Psalm 4:4–5 (MSG)

Rehearsing in your mind how you will respond to anger is one way to short-circuit and alter habitual reactions.

Try it for a month. For the next thirty days maintain an anger journal. Pray every day and ask God to help you before you start writing. Whenever you become aware of anger, irritation, annoyance, rage, etc., grab your anger journal and record the following information:

- Date and time of day.

- Rate the intensity of your anger from 1–10, 1 equaling anger that is barely noticeable, 10 rage that is out of control.

- Try to determine what specifically you are angry about. This may take some real analyzing. It could be a combination of things or one single issue.

- What were the primary emotion/emotions that led to your anger (frustration, hurt, fear, other)?

- Identify any unmet expectations that may have led you to feel angry.

- Describe your behavior both during and after you felt angry.

- How could you handle this situation more effectively in the future?

- What did you want to accomplish?

- Did you implement any plan?

Rehearsing in your mind how you will respond to anger is one way to short-circuit and alter habitual reactions.

Anger letters - Write a letter to yourself identifying what you're angry about, who you are angry at and what you want changed. Pray and ask God to help you before you start writing. Important: be honest. Question: how do I redirect or stop this runaway anger train? I can see it coming but I can't stop it. Answer: You can prepare and practice mentally to resist habitual ways of responding to anger.

Mentally rehearse your anger responses - Rehearsing in your mind how you will respond to anger is one way to short-circuit and alter habitual reactions. Here are a few suggestions: buy yourself some time by delaying your response—take a deep breath or excuse yourself and avoid further engagement but promise to clear the matter at a later time (don't wait too long). Engage a mental trigger-word to stop you from reacting (think, "Lord, help").

> *Rehearsing in your mind how you will respond to anger is one way to short-circuit and alter habitual reactions.*

> *Do not be quickly provoked in your spirit,*
> *for anger resides in the lap of fools.*
> Ecclesiastes 7:9

> *Out of the same mouth come praise and cursing.*
> *My brothers, this should not be.*
> James 3:10

In order to begin the healing process, you've got to bring your anger out into the light.

Helpful reading:
- New Testament, James, Chapter 3
- *Make Anger Your Ally,* by Dr. Neil Clark Warren.

Practice. Pray. Get an accountability partner. Share your successes and failures.

Confess your anger to others. In order to begin the healing process, you've got to bring your anger out into the light. Confess to other safe men your inappropriate anger. *God opposes the proud but gives grace to the humble. Humble yourselves; therefore, under God's mighty hand, that he may lift you up in due time* (1 Peter 5:5–6).

The Verbally Abusive Relationship

In her book *The Verbally Abusive Relationship* (Adams Media, 1996), author Patricia Evans defines this type of relationship as occurring when either words or attitude mistreat, disrespect, or devalue another person. It often manifests itself as an outburst of anger, such as "you are too sensitive," or "I really didn't mean that."

A "verbal abuser" may show some of the following characteristics, in varying degree. Which of these represent you?

Traits of a "verbal abuser"

- ☐ Irritable
- ☐ Blames his spouse for his reactions
- ☐ Unpredictable
- ☐ Angry by nature
- ☐ Uptight
- ☐ Unsympathetic to mate's feelings
- ☐ Demanding and argumentative
- ☐ Controlling nature
- ☐ Silent and very private at times
- ☐ A "nice person" to others
- ☐ Competitive with your mate
- ☐ Overt or very subtle brainwashing
- ☐ Jealous tendencies
- ☐ Explosive reactions
- ☐ Overly-critical nature
- ☐ Manipulative
- ☐ Emotional outbursts; name calling
- ☐ Confrontational; hurtful
- ☐ Does not express feelings
- ☐ Your day is dictated by the emotional abuser's attitude

In many cases where there is verbal abuse, the couple either lacks mutual goals or lacks the ability to discuss their goals in a setting of equality and respect for the relationship.

> **As we grow in self-control and learn to treat others with respect and honor, we become more and more like Jesus Christ.**

POINT TO PONDER

Anger is an energy that offers tremendous potential when it is controlled and put into action creatively.

What will you do this week to start working on your possible abusive behavior?

_____

_____

_____

How could you seek out help and not ignore this problem anymore?

_____

_____

_____

CHAPTER 17

DON'T WASTE YOUR PAIN

As you struggle to understand how you have arrived at this point, to identify and understand the problems and what this pain you're feeling is all about, I encourage you "to make pain your friend."

Many counselors will tell you (rightly so) that most of men's problems stem out of their own arrogance, ignorance, and anger. I believe that this is right. We externalize our anger and arrogance through unkind and unsafe behavior and then reap the consequences of hurting the people around us. The problem is that it is our self-centered behavior (arrogance) that alienates our wives and children from us because it generates fear in the opposite sex and insecurity in our children. Our own arrogance and anger throw our life into a downward spiral, fast and furiously. Everyone ends up getting hurt.

Be proactive in your efforts to understand how you got here and what you can do to begin healing. Ask yourself:

1. **What does it mean to make pain your friend?**

2. **How can your pain be used for the good of those involved?**

3. **What is God's purpose in this season of pain?**

Pain is a wake up call that tells you that something is wrong. In that way, it can be your partner in healing. You must recognize the pain and find its root as well as its purpose. There is "good pain" (useful and fruitful) and there is "bad pain" (useless and detrimental). You need to distinguish the difference between the good pain and the bad pain.

The Path to Healing

The chart below marks your crisis, your struggles, your eventual surrender to God, and the path this process generally follows. Use it often to guide and trace your own progress toward healing.

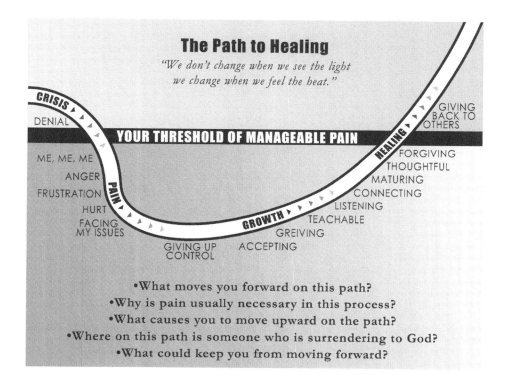

The Path to Healing

"We don't change when we see the light we change when we feel the heat."

CRISIS
DENIAL

YOUR THRESHOLD OF MANAGEABLE PAIN

ME, ME, ME
ANGER
FRUSTRATION
HURT
FACING
MY ISSUES

GIVING UP CONTROL   ACCEPTING

PAIN

GROWTH   TEACHABLE
GREIVING

HEALING

GIVING BACK TO OTHERS

FORGIVING
THOUGHTFUL
MATURING
CONNECTING
LISTENING

•What moves you forward on this path?
•Why is pain usually necessary in this process?
•What causes you to move upward on the path?
•Where on this path is someone who is surrendering to God?
•What could keep you from moving forward?

Bad Pain vs. Good Pain

First, the bad pain

Bad pain produces no growth. We repeat old patterns, avoid change, or stay in the victim role. We refuse to face our part where growth is concerned. Simply, it is wasted pain. It's "good for nothing" pain.

Bad pain is pain that produces no growth. We repeat old patterns, avoid change, or stay in the victim role.

In their book *How People Grow* (Zondervan 2004), Drs. Henry Cloud and John Townsend tell us bad pain is like this verse:

As a dog returns to its vomit, so a fool repeats his folly.
Proverbs 26:11

Now the Good Pain

Yes, pain can be good. Good pain is all about embracing what hurts in order to grow, reaching for a higher level, drawing closer to God and developing your character. It's about choosing not to stay in the "pity party" pattern, but rather seeing where you are realistically, then evaluating, grieving, and facing the situation head on.

Drs. Cloud and Townsend tell us: "Suffering can be good. It can take us to places where one or more seasons of 'comfort' cannot."

Here's a slogan from *Men on the Edge*: "The Edge of the Cliff" is the right place to be if you want to grow. Any other place seems irrelevant to your current pain. Any place other than "The Edge" does not attract your attention strongly enough because of the lack of pain there. In the absence of pain, there is no reason to grow because we are comfortable, so we resist change. Our nature seeks for comfort, while the Holy Spirit searches for character. Character comes through pain. Therefore, "no pain, no gain" is true in this season of your life. The "Edge of the Cliff" is where you will begin to grow. If you want a better outcome than what you've had so far, you must face the pain head on. Start from "The Edge." There is no better place for you to be if you want to grow. Just don't stay there for too long. You need to learn how to move on.

We also rejoice in our sufferings, because we know that suffering produces perseverance; perseverance, character; and character, hope.
Romans 5:3

POINT TO PONDER

Suffering can be good. It can take us to places where seasons of "comfort" cannot.

Do you believe that God has a purpose for your pain? If so, what do you think it is?

_____

_____

_____

CHAPTER 18

GRIEVING HURTS, HANG-UPS AND HABITS

What is it to grieve?

Grieving is a process. A person who has been hurt needs to go through it in order to move on in a healthy way. Its purpose is to lead the hurting to healing, forgiveness, and eventually reconciliation, whenever possible. Grief is hard and encompasses experiences of emotions such as pain, denial, ambivalence, revenge, indifference, and more. These emotions don't necessarily happen in the order presented here; they don't come at you individually either. Sometimes it's all at once—a "when it rains, it pours" kind of experience. At other times, you may feel blocked for days, weeks, months, or even years. Grief is a necessary process for health. Even Jesus went through it.

When you get offended in life, you have the choice to opt for a path that will lead to health, or a path that will be unhealthy. The unhealthy path will lead you to negative emotions. These will eventually have negative repercussions in your relationships, such as bitterness or depression. People who seek the unhealthy path risk going even further by seeking revenge or denying the offender the freedom that Jesus came to offer: forgiveness! They run away from the causes of the pain and will typically become either depressed or bitter. Those who are willing to face the facts in a biblical and intelligent manner, while surrendering to God's principles and precepts, will eventually initiate the grieving process and choose a healthy pathway.

When Jesus heard about John the Baptist's beheading, he withdrew from the crowds in order to grieve. Jesus sought solitude after the news of John's death. Sometimes we may need to deal with our grief alone. Jesus did not dwell on his grief, but returned to the ministry he came to do (see Matthew 14:13–14).

Sometimes you grieve privately and sometimes you need a support group around you such as a Men On the Edge group (www.MenOnTheEdge.com). If you are looking for a grief support group, see if your local church offers such a service or see www.griefshare.org. Many churches have a 12-step program called Celebrate Recovery to help people grieve and recover from hurts, hang-ups, and habits. Here's an excerpt from this ministry's website: **Celebrate Recovery's Eight Recovery Principles:** *The Road to Recovery, Based on the Beatitudes:*

Celebrate Recovery - The Road to Recovery

Realize I'm not God; I admit that I am powerless to control my tendency to do the wrong thing and that my life is unmanageable. (Step 1)

Happy are those who know that they are spiritually poor.

Earnestly believe that God exists, that I matter to him and that he has the power to help me recover. (Step 2)

Happy are those who mourn, for they shall be comforted.

Consciously choose to commit all my life and will to Christ's care and control. (Step 3)

Happy are the meek.

Openly examine and confess my faults to myself, to God, and to someone I trust. (Steps 4 and 5)

Happy are the pure in heart.

Voluntarily submit to any and all changes God wants to make in my life and humbly ask him to remove my character defects. (Steps 6 and 7)

Happy are those whose greatest desire is to do what God requires.

Evaluate all my relationships. Offer forgiveness to those who have hurt me and make amends for harm I've done to others when possible, except when to do so would harm them or others. (Steps 8 and 9)

Happy are the merciful. Happy are the peacemakers.

Reserve a time with God for self-examination, Bible reading, and prayer in order to know God and his will for my life and to gain the power to follow his will. (Steps 10 and 11)

Yield myself to God to be used to bring this Good News to others, both by my example and my words. (Step 12)

Visit **celebraterecovery.com.** Celebrate Recovery is an amazing process and support for hurting people—all people.

Pain is about "picking up your cross" and owning your responsibility for growth. At the "Edge of the Cliff," we commit to grow in the midst of an unfair situation within a broken world, to arrive at a better outcome. At the "Edge of the Cliff" it is permissible to grieve the hurts, hang-ups and habits and watch as the fruit of character begins to develop in the midst of a crisis. Grief is a frequent companion to pain. Below is a chart designed to help you understand the process of dealing with and recovering from a crisis. Know for now that asking questions, digging deep for the truth and soul searching—no matter how painful it is to do—will in time, give way to God's freedom.

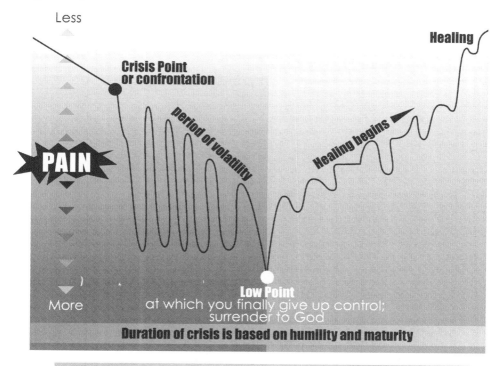

> **Ultimately, God is more interested in your character than in your comfort.**

God uses your circumstances—the good, the bad and the ugly, to refine your character. How can you use your pain to develop a Christ-like character? God sees you as a "diamond in the rough." He sees that "big P" in you—potential. But in order for you to get to the diamond (your potential), you have to go into the diamond mine and get dirty while you are searching in the rough. That's the journey. Get dirty and find the refined character God is forming in you, while you are getting dirty and hurting in the process. If you seek freedom, you must face Truth. Jesus said in John 8:32 *You will know the truth and the truth will set you free* (GW). Jesus himself is the truth that sets us completely free. John 8:36 says, *So if the Son sets you free, you will be absolutely free.* He is the source of truth, the perfect standard of what is right. He frees us from the consequences of sin, from self-deception and from deception by Satan. He shows us clearly the way to eternal life with God. Jesus does not give us freedom to do what we want, but freedom to follow God. As we seek to serve God, Jesus' perfect truth frees us to be all that God meant us to be.

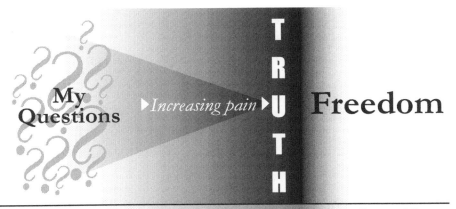

What pains have caused you to deny or avoid God's truth?

- Childhood hurts
- Loneliness
- Controlling behavior
- Codependency
- Depression

- Insecurities
- Helplessness
- Inadequacy
- Disappointment
- Emptiness

- Character flaws
- Brokenness
- Self-centeredness
- Blaming Others
- Fear or Rejection

- Addiction
- Betrayal
- Loss
- Rage
- Envy

Then you will know the truth, and the truth will set you free.
John 8:32

If you want to know who you are and why you have suffered, get into God's word and God's will. Do this in prayer, in fellowship with other Christians, and through a support group or Bible study in your church.

- Where is God leading you?
- What does God want you to learn?
- What does God want you to do?

> *God is waiting to help us, but before he can, we've got to*
> *release our grip on all those other things*
> *we think will help us.*

Holding On at the Edge of the Cliff

Once there was a man who had fallen from the edge of a cliff. On his way down, he got hold of a branch and was hanging on to it for his life.

"Help! Help!" he cried, hoping someone walking by would hear him.

"Help! Help! HELP!" His cries became more frantic, but there was no answer. After several more attempts to get someone's attention, at last he heard, "Yes, yes, I am here."

The man shouted again, "Can you help me?"

"Yes," God finally answered, "I can help you. But before I can help you, you must let go of the branch."

"Are you kidding?" the man said.

"Don't trust the branch, trust Me…I created that branch so that you would call on me for help."

Dismayed, the man called out, "Is there anyone else out there?"

Often we live life placing our trust and confidence in the things that God has created, rather than on God himself. What are you trusting in? Your self-confidence? Your self-sufficiency? A past achievement? A person? (Who?) Get away from that kind of thinking, which got you to the edge of the cliff, and let go of the branch. Let go and let God! Trust in God. In the Bible, in John 14:6, God says, *I am the way, the truth and the life, no one comes to the father, except through me.*

Believe it or not, most of our growth is done on the edge of the cliff. God is waiting to help us, but before he can, we've got to release our grip on all those other things we think will help us. When we do, we'll drop into God's waiting arms.

Believe it or not, most of our growth is done on the edge of the cliff.

It's human nature to think that God isn't moving fast enough for us. He isn't doing it our way and in our timeframe. We sometimes see God as a distant genie in the sky or mythical genie in a bottle.

And the problem is that our genie in the sky isn't saving us out of our physical situation fast enough. But God is not a genie in the sky. He is a loving Father who knows exactly what we need in order to grow into the likeness of his Son and he promises to meet our very needs. Philippians 4:19 reads, "And my God will meet all your needs according to his glorious riches in Christ Jesus." God is not a spiritual vending machine, in which you put in a coin of good behavior for the next hour and expect an instant visible result or solution. God is an intimate father who cares about your very being. That brings us to another issue: we expect God to *physically* save us, just as the Jews did in Jesus' time. But Jesus did not come to physically save us. Rather, he came to save us spiritually. There is, however, an added physical reward to that spiritual salvation: Once we are spiritually safe (asked God for forgiveness and recognize Jesus' atonement for our sins), God equips us with a supernatural power (God's Spirit to dwell in us) in order to help us get off the "edge of the cliff." That power is the fruit that we show when we are saved. The fruit of the Spirit, as explained in chapter 5, takes you off the edge of the cliff. When your behavior displays the flavors of love, joy, peace, patience, kindness, goodness, faithfulness, humility, and self-control, you will produce fruit in your character. That character will come through in your behavior and relationships to others. Relationships will be healed. That is where the truth sets you free, physically.

We sometimes see God as a distant genie in the sky or mythical genie in a bottle.

Hanging on the edge of the cliff is the place from where you will start to grow. When you have no one else to depend on, nowhere else to hide, you finally realize that God is all you need—because God is all you've got.

You need to use the little faith you have in order to let go. Maybe you won't need more than a mustard seed-sized faith. The secret is putting a small faith in a big God. Once you realize that God caught you from falling, your faith will increase and you will learn to live by faith and not by sight. Hebrews 11:1 says, *Now faith is being sure of what we hope for and certain of what we do not see.*

God is just waiting to save you and reconnect with you. He literally died for this to happen. So if you let go of that branch you are clinging to, God will catch you. When you trust him to do what's best for you, he will transform your heart. When you let go and let God, he will change you from the inside out.

> *I must get out of his way and let him work, let go of control and let God control.*

You must let God take control of your marriage, your wife, your kids, your growth, your personal problems, and the way you respond to those problems. Turning over all the areas of your life to God and leaving the problems in the "God box" is what is called surrender. Making Jesus your savior is good and leads the way to growth. You can now also make him your Lord by surrendering it all to him. You must get out of his way and let him work, let go of control and let God control.

The more I learned, the more I realized, I didn't know very much. When I was young, I thought I was the captain of my life—at the wheel and in complete control. Now I know that I have very little control over anything in life. So don't be afraid of the pain. Instead, welcome it.

> *God uses pain to teach us lessons of life. Pain can be a powerful motivator.*

POINT TO PONDER

Hanging on the edge of the cliff is the place from where you will start to grow. When you have no one else to depend on, nowhere else to hide, you finally realize that God is all you need—because God is all you've got.

What is the purpose of your grief?

_____

_____

_____

CHAPTER 19

THE PURPOSE OF PAIN

What is the Difference Between Trials and Temptations?

James 1:12 tells us, *Blessed is the man who perseveres under trial, because when he has stood the test, he will receive the crown of life that God has promised to those who love him.* James uses a word that can be translated as "trials" or "temptations." Both words have the same root in Greek but are very different by design and purpose. Trials are designed by God to develop your character. Temptations are designed by Satan to cause you to sin and alienate you from God. James says that if you resist temptations or if you overcome trials, a crown of life awaits you. That is the essence of the abundant life Jesus talks about in John 10:10.

> God's purpose for our trials is life. Satan's purpose for our temptations is death.

If you don't overcome trials or resist temptations, you will give in to sin, as explained in later verses: *But each one is tempted when, by his own evil desire, he is dragged away and enticed. Then, after desire has conceived, it gives birth to sin; and sin, when it is full-grown, gives birth to death* (James 1:14–15).

God's purpose for our trials is life. Satan's purpose for our temptations is death. You must learn to distinguish what is coming at you so you know how to react when it comes knocking at the door of your life and relationships.

See God's Purpose in Your Pain

One weekend several years back, my pastor, Rick Warren, preached on pain. I was gripped by the message he delivered, because he'd found a positive point in pain and encouraged us to look for God's purpose in our problems.

1. God uses pain to direct us

When we look to God in the midst of our pain, we'll find he leads us one step at a time to where he wants us to be. It's all about trusting him even when it hurts. We must keep the truth that God did not cause our pain at the forefront of our minds…and he will use it for good when we trust our lives into his keeping. Paul explained to the Corinthians that their pain was used by God to redirect their focus from the bad stuff to him. It caused them all to rejoice.

I am glad…not because it hurt you but because the pain turned you to God…
2 Corinthians 7:9 (TLB)

Ask God, "Lord, do I have a heart problem?"

2. God uses pain to inspect us

Why should God need to inspect us? you might ask. *Didn't he make us? Doesn't he already know everything about us?* Well, yes, he does. But the problem is that we often don't know ourselves. God does indeed know all about us and he knows that in order for us to let go of our pains, we've got to first know ourselves. How can we let go of something we don't know we're holding on to? The only way we can grow to be more like Jesus is when we see ourselves in the light of his truth. So ask God, "Lord, do I have a heart problem?"

[The Lord] searches our hearts and examines our deepest motives so he can give to each person his right reward, according to his deeds— how he has lived. Jeremiah 17:10 (TLB)

You [God] inspect them every morning and test them every minute. Job 7:18 (TEV)

3. God uses pain to correct us

When you were a child, you probably hated getting a spanking or some other punishment for your misbehavior. Yet later, when you had a little more sense, you realized that without that discipline, you might have gone right on walking into trouble—and it would only have gotten worse. So that discipline, painful as it may have been, actually served to correct the course you were on. The author of Hebrews reminds us how important it is to accept God's correction as proof of his love for his children. It is an encouragement, an evidence of his love.

*My son, do not make light of the Lord's discipline, and do not lose
heart when he rebukes you, because the Lord disciplines those he loves,
and he punishes everyone he accepts as a son. Endure hardship as
discipline; God is treating you as sons. For what son is not disciplined
by his father?* Hebrews 12:5–7

God often allows pain to show us the value of his love. In the
Beatitudes, Jesus said: *You're blessed when you feel you've lost what is most dear to
you. Only then can you be embraced by the One most dear to you"* (Matthew 5:4 MSG).
The One is Jesus. It's the same in our walk with God. He often allows pain
to help us learn about ourselves, about him, or about what we should be
doing. He also uses pain to develop our character and learn our weaknesses.
So when you experience pain, think of it as God wanting you to
understanding something in regards to the value of pain. After the pain,
you will be comforted by his love. His motive for correcting us is his love
for us. It is a privilege to be disciplined by God. Those who don't know
God can only be "disciplined" by the world and the sins of others, which
bear no fruit. Therefore being corrected by God is a privilege. While you
are in pain, it may be hard to grasp. Don't ask God "why." Ask "what."
Ask "what" God is doing.

God often allows pain to help us learn something about ourselves,
about him or about what we should be doing.

*God corrects all of his children and if he doesn't correct you, then
you don't really belong to him…God corrects us for our own good,
because he wants us to be holy, as he is.* Hebrews 12:8, 10 (CEV)

4. God uses pain to protect us

I was one of those kids who would always climb a little higher or
wander off a little further than my parents wanted me to. As a result, I
would fall or get lost now and then. Once I lost track of my folks in a
baseball stadium—crowds everywhere and of course, I didn't have my
ticket stub so no one knew how to help me to get back to my seat. It was
many years ago, but I remember well how scared I was. Finally, a man who
worked at the stadium said he had an idea. They put a message on the big
scoreboard in the outfield and after what seemed like a long time, my
parents came and found me.

"Now Gary," my dad said after giving me a big hug, "why did you
wander off? What do we always tell you about staying right next to Mom

and Dad?" I hadn't quite gotten it before that day, but I never forgot it after that day. Because of my pain and fear, getting lost in a gigantic baseball stadium, I learned that my parents only wanted to protect me.

Maybe you've missed a flight and found yourself irritated with the inconvenience, only to learn later that your business appointment was canceled anyway. Perhaps you've been late for work or caught in a traffic jam that turned out to be "a blessing in disguise." Sometimes, God allows pain in our lives to simply protect us from far bigger problems.

> *God is leading you away from danger, giving you freedom.*
> Job 36:16 (NLT)

5. God uses pain to perfect us.

Most of us—especially men—are neither inclined nor open to change. We think we're just fine the way we are and if anyone else doesn't like it, that's their problem. Does that sound familiar? Have you ever reevaluated your life after a painful experience? Pain allows you to refocus and reassess. It even refines you and your faith. *Pure gold put in the fire comes out of it proved pure; genuine faith put through this suffering comes out proved genuine. When Jesus wraps this all up, it's your faith, not your gold that God will have on display as evidence of his victory* (1 Peter 1:7 MSG).

Maybe it was the "F" you got in math that made you work harder to graduate, or the job you lost that made you learn new skills to get a better job. We usually only change when we're forced to, when maintaining the status quo becomes too uncomfortable. So God, whose goal is to change us into the likeness of his Son, who knows how far we are from that goal, will allow pain to get us to change and rethink. Would you consider that this is exactly what God wants from you in this instance of marital challenges? He wants you to listen, to pay attention, and to surrender your will so that you will redirect your life and align it with *his* will.

We usually only change when we are forced to, when maintaining the status quo becomes too uncomfortable.

> *After you have suffered for a little while, the God of all grace, who calls you to share his eternal glory in union with Christ, will himself perfect you and give you firmness, strength and a sure foundation.*
> 1 Peter 5:10 (TEV)

The key to moving forward is to:
- **Be real – Face the facts**
- **Be honest – Accept the facts**
- **Be transparent – Share the facts**

Be open about your feelings - Author C.S. Lewis said, "God whispers to us in our pleasures, but shouts in our pain."

Be humble about your faults - We usually resist change until the pain is greater than the fear of change.

Be frank about your failures - Until you can admit your sins, you cannot repent, cannot be helped. *Christ Jesus came into the world to save sinners—of whom I am the worst* (1 Timothy 1:15).

Be honest about your frustrations - God isn't surprised by anything in your life or any negative feeling you are harboring. When you admit it, then you can begin to let go, and start healing.

Be truthful about your limitations - *Although I have the desire to do what is right, I don't do it...Instead, I do the evil that I don't want to do.* (Romans 7:18–19 GW)

Be candid about your fears - Life is too short to make all the mistakes yourself. God gives us pain to protect us, inspect us, and correct us.

Questions to ponder:
- [ ] **Where does God want to direct you?**
- [ ] **What does God want to inspect in you?**
- [ ] **What correction do you need from God?**
- [ ] **What is God protecting you from?**
- [ ] **Which part of your character is God wanting to perfect?**

Allow other people to come alongside you, so that they can point out a potential "blind spot" and help you get up when you fall.

> *Two people are better than one... If one falls down, the other can help him up. But it is bad for the person who is alone and falls, because no one is there to help.* Ecclesiastes 4:9–10 (NCV)

There is nothing we can't learn if we simply ask the right questions. So instead of asking "Why me, God?," try asking: "Lord, what do you want me to learn? What can I do to be proactive in this situation?" Taking a good hard look at ourselves in the mirror may be uncomfortable, but more often than not, it's necessary. So think of it this way: instead of focusing on yourself, look at what God wants you to see. Second Corinthians 1:4–6 says, *[God] comforts us in all our troubles so that we can comfort others. When they are troubled, we will be able to give them the same comfort God has given us* (NLT).

Many men have had to learn all this the hard way. It is probably time for you to start growing up. Start making better decisions. Be a man of your word. Stop living for comfort and pleasure and let God make you a man of character. In a generation starved of integrity, become a man of God; build a strong character, one experience at a time. If you love God, you will obey him. Jesus said in John 14:21, *The one who obeys me is the one who loves me; and because he loves me, my Father will love him; and I will too, and I will reveal myself to him* (TLB).

To be like Christ we have to endure pain, suffering, and hurt. Like he needed to be broken in order to redeem our sins, we need to be broken also. We need to remember this truth, every single day: "I'll never really be 100 percent comfortable this side of Heaven."

And if children, then heirs—heirs of God and joint heirs with Christ, if indeed we suffer with Him, that we may also be glorified together. Romans 8:17 (NKJV)

Suffering gives God an opportunity to display God's work in you.

Your attitude should be the same as that of Christ Jesus.
Philippians 2:5

God will take us through our own wilderness experiences so that we can in turn learn how to help others through our past painful experiences.

...God of all comfort, who comforts us in all our troubles, so that we can comfort those in any trouble with the comfort we ourselves have received from God. 2 Corinthians 1:3–4

To grow, which of these healthy choices do you need to apply to your life?

- ☐ **A new attitude**
- ☐ **Learn to listen to God**
- ☐ **Learn to trust God**
- ☐ **Choose godly friends**
- ☐ **Learn to live life God's way**

- [ ] **Learn to make the most of every situation**
- [ ] **Spend time reading the Bible daily**
- [ ] **Learn to use other men for accountability**

Do you want God to be looking down on you, saying, "That's my boy; that's my son"? He will, if you are making these healthy choices—his choices.

> *His master praised him for good work. "You have been faithful in handling this small amount," he told him, "so now I will give you many more responsibilities. Begin the joyous tasks I have assigned to you."*
> Matthew 25:21 (TLB)

Claiming Victory in a Season of Suffering

None of us look forward to suffering or pain. We may not understand what is happening to us or why it is happening, but we can thankfully trust in the knowledge that we have a Lord and Savior who sees the big picture. He knows why we are suffering. And not only does he use our suffering to claim victory, he will lovingly carry us through these times and work miracles in our lives if we allow him to.

If God loves us, why does he allow us to suffer?

> *God uses our suffering to conquer sin, to bring about a greater good, or prevent a greater evil.*

The truth is that God does allow suffering. However, God never allows us to suffer needlessly. He always has a purpose and will use our suffering for good if we surrender it to him.

As examples, God may use your suffering for the following purposes:

- [ ] **God uses our suffering to draw us closer to him.**

> *To this you were called, because Christ suffered for you, leaving you an example, that you should follow in his steps.*
> 1 Peter 2:21

> *We must go through many hardships to enter the kingdom of God.*
> Acts 14:22

> *That is why, for Christ's sake, I delight in weakness, in insults, in hardships, in persecutions, in difficulties. For when I am weak, then I am strong.*
> 2 Corinthians 12:10

☐ **God uses our suffering to conquer sin, to bring about a greater good, or prevent a greater evil.**

So then, since Christ suffered physical pain, you must arm yourselves with the same attitude he had, and be ready to suffer, too. For if you have suffered physically for Christ, you have finished with sin.
1 Peter 4:1 (NLT)

But if Christ is in you, your body is dead because of sin, yet your spirit is alive because of righteousness. Romans 8:10

Study in the books of Job and Jonah how God used their suffering—and even their disobedience—to bring about a greater good.

☐ **God uses our suffering for the healing of others.**

So then, those who suffer according to God's will should commit themselves to their faithful Creator and continue to do good.
1 Peter 4:19

Praise be to the God and Father of our Lord Jesus Christ, the Father of compassion and the God of all comfort, who comforts us in all our troubles, so that we can comfort those in any trouble with the comfort we ourselves have received from God.
2 Corinthians 1:3–4

So in fact, when we surrender our pain and suffering to God, he heals us from our suffering and he uses our bruised hearts to heal others. If we understand that there is purpose in our suffering, take comfort in God's promises, and surrender our suffering to him, then not only can we be healed, but we can also be used by God.

> **When we surrender our pain and suffering to God, not only does He heal us from our suffering, but he uses our bruised hearts to heal others.**

No discipline seems pleasant at the time, but painful. Later on, however, it produces a harvest of righteousness and peace for those who have been trained by it. Hebrews 12:11

POINT TO PONDER

God often allows pain to help us learn something about ourselves, about him, or about what we should be doing.

What is the purpose for your pain?

_____

_____

_____

CHAPTER 20

THE DIAMOND IN THE ROUGH

Does God See You As a Diamond in the Rough?

If you take situations in life out of God's hands or try to change God's plan, what does it do for you? Are you cheating the God system, are you bypassing the lesson God wants you to learn? If you do not face the pain, the hurt, the anger, and the frustrations head on, you will find that they will come back in through the "back door" or the "side door." You will eventually have to deal with it. Trying to take the situation (your marriage, your problems) out of God's hands and manipulating the situation for your own hidden agenda will show that you are really not trusting God. *Blessed is the man who preserves under trial, because when he has stood the test, he will receive the crown of life that God has promised to those who love him*, says James 1:12.

Are you cheating the God system, are you bypassing the lesson that God wants you to learn?

Men, we've got to learn the following truth: If you really want to mess up the situation, just try to take full control of your problems by yourself and leave God out of them. It never works. How can we truly know the depth of our character except under the fire, in the midst of our crisis?

Put on a positive attitude. Step out in faith and determine that, whatever you are facing, you will give the situation to God. You will surrender the situation to God, confident that you will ultimately benefit from that move. You will grow and your character will be developed—and that means that you win, God wins and so do all other people involved. *"For I know the plans I have for you," declares the Lord, "plans to prosper you and not to harm you, plans to give you hope and a future,"* says Jeremiah 29:11.

> *If you really want to mess up the situation, just try to take full control of your problems by yourself and leave God out of them.*

When God looks at you, he sees the big "P"—for potential. You might see yourself as a piece of charcoal in the dirt. But God sees you as all that you can be—a diamond in the rough. He doesn't look at the outward appearance because the outward appearance deceives.

The fact is that God *cannot* be deceived. He doesn't even need to look at your outward appearance—he looks at your heart. In 1 Samuel 16:7 God says, *Pay no attention to how tall and handsome he is. I have rejected him, because I do not judge as people judge. They look at the outward appearance, but I look at the heart* (TEV).

Learn to thank God for his loving grace and renewing mercy. Thank him that he forgave you, in spite of who you are and what you have done. Grace, defined, is unmerited favor, which means undeserved forgiveness.

When you pray to God, ask him to take your shortcomings, your faults, your deep, deep wounds, your hurts and insecurities—and ask him to heal you. Ask him to guide you to become the godly man he has created you to be. May he show you the things you need to work on and change you, no matter what it takes. Challenge the Lord to change you.

Over time, as you work through these changes, you will learn what you are all about. It is said that "character is who you are when no one is looking." Are you an angry person? Are you bitter toward those around you? Are you irritating to those you touch in your daily life? Who *are* you—when no one is looking?

Do You Like the Man in Your Mirror?

For so many years, when I took that daily look I didn't like what I saw. I wanted to be respected and looked up to. But self-help programs and books only led to more failure. I was so tired of failing, so worn out from beating my head against the wall. I knew I had to change. At long last the moment came when I knew I had to choose to live God's way.

The challenge is that when we look at God's law, we try to obey it and thus try by our human efforts to become more "holy." This is wrong thinking. Holiness comes through changing the way we think. *Do not conform any longer to the pattern of this world, but be transformed by the renewing of your mind. Then you will be able to test and approve what God's will is—his good, pleasing and perfect will,* says Romans 12:2.

The Word of God is compared to a mirror. You see, God never intended man to be able to keep up with the law and obey it all. He gave it to us so that it would reflect our inability to fulfill it. When we honestly look at the law, we can see that we are not capable of keeping it and therefore (if we are honest) we will admit we need God. That takes honesty and humility. That is where God wants us. Once you are honest and humble, God can start to change you because now, you have earnestly admitted that you need him. Then you become the diamond in the rough.

It says in the book of James that anyone who does not apply changes to how he lives when he hears the Word of God is like a man who looks at himself in a mirror and then forgets what he saw. James 1:22–24 says, *Do not merely listen to the word and so deceive yourselves. Do what it says. Anyone who listens to the word but does not do what it says is like a man who looks at his face in a mirror and, after looking at himself, goes away and immediately forgets what he looks like.*

When you look into a mirror, you can do it in two different ways:

1. **You glance and move on.**
2. **You look and glean.**

When you wake up in the morning and look into the mirror, it is with the intent of seeing the "damage" from the night before. Hopefully you will also do something about it to change your appearance before you walk out the door—comb your hair, brush your teeth, etc.

A mirror reveals your outward appearance, but the Word of God (The Bible) reveals your inward appearance. You still need to apply some change. So, when the Word of God tells you the condition of your heart, you understand that you need to apply changes to your character, your thinking, and your behavior. That is one of the reasons why some people don't like to read the Bible...they are afraid of seeing themselves or unwilling to accept the truth about themselves and then make appropriate changes. As long as you are afraid to face the truth, you will need to see a counselor. Once you know the truth and are able to accept it, it will set you free and you will be free indeed. John 8:32 says, *Then you will know the truth and the truth will set you free.*

> **As long as you are afraid to face the truth,**
> **you will need to see a counselor.**

For God so loved the world that he gave his one and only Son, that whoever believes in him shall not perish but have eternal life.
John 3:16

When you come to that place of struggling with a choice, close your eyes for a moment and visualize the cross with Christ nailed to it. God took your pain—all of it. He paid the price once and for all. God will be there for you. Just believe.

Are you afraid that reading the Bible will reveal "the real you"?

Will you trust God with all areas of your life?

I will never leave you nor forsake you.
Hebrews 13:5 (NKJV)

> **When you come to that place of struggling with a choice,**
> **close your eyes for a moment and visualize the cross with**
> **Christ nailed to it. God took your pain—all of it.**

POINT TO PONDER

If you really want to mess up the situation, just try to take full control of your problems by yourself and leave God out of them.

Will there be a right reason or time to give up?

_____

_____

_____

As we close this volume, I'd like to leave you with these last thoughts:

THE MORE I KNOW

- The statement "I just need to be happy" doesn't mean you leave.
- The male human species can be dense between the left and right ears.
- You can win the battle, but lose the war.
- The more I know, the more I realize I don't know.
- The more I know, the more I realize I don't ask for help until it's almost too late.
- The more I know, the more I realize it's more about me than it is about her.
- The more I know, the more I know it's OK to say sorry, even when…
- The more I know, I pray "Lord show me what I need to know."
- The more I know, the more I realize love is an action, not a tone of voice.
- The more I know, pride and selfishness don't taste very good.
- I've learned that love is a committed, day-by-day, twinkle in your eye kind of thing.
- I've learned that love is staying in the relationship, even when you don't feel like it.
- I've learned that love is saying you're sorry, meaning it and not doing it again.
- I've learned that I can make a difference, if I don't give up.
- I've learned that only prayer can move the mountain in front of me; control and manipulation is not the answer.
- I've learned that you can't make someone love you, you can only love them.
- I've learned that I can't change others, only God can.
- The more I know, the more I realize that only God can fill this emptiness inside of me.
- The more I know, the more I realize God's perspective doesn't always make sense to me. Life is not about what you know, but about who you trust and obey.

Bibliography

The Dance of Anger: A Woman's Guide to Changing the Patterns of Intimate Relationships, by Harriet Lerner, Harper Paperbacks 2005.

How People Grow: What the Bible Reveals About Personal Growth, by Drs. Henry Cloud and John Townsend, Zondervan, 2004.

Make Anger Your Ally: Harnessing Our Most Baffling Emotion, by Neil Clark Warren, Doubleday, 1985.

The Purpose Driven Life, by Rick Warren, Zondervan, 2002.

The Seven Habits of Highly Effective People, by Stephen Covey, Simon & Schuster, 1989.

10 Great Dates to Energize Your Marriage, by David and Claudia Arp, Zondervan 1997.

The Verbally Abusive Relationship: How to Recognize It and How to Respond, by Patricia Evans, Adams Media, 1996.

My intention with this book has been to help you understand a little more about what marriage means to both you and your wife, as well as what steps you can take to get out of the marital challenges you currently find yourself in. If you desire to go deeper into applying the steps you need to take, please look for *Men on the Edge, Book Two: Digging Deeper,* due to be released in the near future. In that book, we'll examine the tools available to help you through your crisis. Please know that you do not have to go through this season alone. God wants you on his team.

About the Author
Gary Hoffman

Gary Hoffman is a marital crisis survivor and leader of the Men on the Edge ministry at Saddleback Church in Lake Forest, CA. "While I regret that my past marriage failed," Gary says, "I am grateful for the lessons learned through my painful trials—principles I bring to my present marriage every day, and have delivered with confidence to men in relationship crisis over the past sixteen years." This book you now hold is based on this marriage-saving wisdom and godly principles, condensed in these valuable lessons.

"Change is hard for all of us and life is often painful," Gary adds, "but I want you to know unequivocally that divorce is not the answer. No matter what she is doing or not doing, ask yourself what is your part in this? In dealing with men for several years, I've learned that most men are not talking to others and often not transparent with others. Instead, they are often focusing on the wrong things in life. I encourage you to learn what God wants to show you in your challenging season!"

If you would like to start a Men on the Edge group of your own, or desire someone to speak at your church or ministry venue, please:

Contact Gary, ghoffman@menontheedge.com
Or contact Jim Zoval, jzoval@menontheedge.com
Both can be reached at:
949-709-7401
PO Box 283
Trabuco Canyon, CA 92678
www.MenOnTheEdge.com

Men on the Edge
Quick Order Form

To order online go to www.MenOnTheEdge.com.

Please send the following books and workbooks:

Title	Qty	Price
❏ Don't Give Up Book, $12.98	____	_____
❏ Don't Give Up Workbook, $9.98	____	_____
❏ Leader Guide: Leadership Secrets to Success, $11.98	____	_____

Sub-total _____

Add 8.75% for shipments to California _____

Shipping: Any 2 books $5.00,

      3 or more books, contact us (see below) _____

Order Total _____

PLEASE PRINT

Name:_____

Address:_____

City:_____ State:_____ Zipcode:_____

Phone:_____

E-mail:_____

Mail Orders with payment to:
    Men on the Edge
    PO Box 283
    Trabuco Canyon, CA 92678

Please send me FREE information on:

❏ Other Books   ❏ Speaking/Seminars

❏ Consulting   ❏ A Group Near Me

❏ Starting a Group

For volume shipping and book order quotes, e-mail
ghoffman@menontheedge.com.

Fax requests for information to: 949-951-0667.
To order online go to www.MenOnTheEdge.com.

Men on the Edge
Quick Order Form

To order online go to www.MenOnTheEdge.com.

Please send the following books and workbooks:

Title	Qty	Price
❑ Don't Give Up Book, $12.98	____	_____
❑ Don't Give Up Workbook, $9.98	____	_____
❑ Leader Guide: Leadership Secrets to Success, $11.98	____	_____

Sub-total _____

Add 8.75% for shipments to California _____

Shipping: Any 2 books $5.00,

         3 or more books, contact us (see below) _____

Order Total _____

PLEASE PRINT

Name:_____

Address:_____

City:_____ State:_____ Zipcode:_____

Phone:_____

E-mail:_____

Mail Orders with payment to:
   Men on the Edge
   PO Box 283
   Trabuco Canyon, CA 92678

Please send me FREE information on:

❑ Other Books   ❑ Speaking/Seminars

❑ Consulting   ❑ A Group Near Me

❑ Starting a Group

For volume shipping and book order quotes, e-mail ghoffman@menontheedge.com.

Fax requests for information to: 949-951-0667
To order online go to www.MenOnTheEdge.com

Made in the USA
Charleston, SC
13 July 2012